Almost
A DARK VALENTINE
NOVELLA SERIES

ALMOST
chosen

SARA MCCLAFLIN

First Edition

ASIN: B0FFZZMYNM

ISBN (trade): 979-8-9991778-3-4

Book Cover: Pia

Editing: Brandy Gibson

Social Media Coordinator: Tawny Gratto

Social Media Group Moderator: Ashley Sullivan

PA: Sarah Toon

Marketing & PR: Wildfire Marketing Solutions

Content Warning

This book contains mature content and situations intended for adult readers (18+). Some of the events, conflicts, or character backstories may touch on sensitive topics.

Reader discretion is strongly advised.

If you'd like to see a detailed list of possible triggers and content notes before you begin, I've prepared one for you and it is located at the back of the book.

CHAPTER ONE

Eden

I walk toward the light.

Not *that* light—the sunlight streaming through the front door of Ink & Stems, the little shop I co-own with my best friend, Willa, in the smallest town God ever put on this side of the Mississippi.

It's my morning to open. I'm the Ink. Calligraphy, signage, invitations. If it needs words, I write it. Every card in a hundred mile radius probably came from my desk.

The Stems? That's all Willa. Florist extraordinaire. Business brain. Creative genius.

She makes everything look easy, and together, we're the kind of pair people trust with their "I do's," baby showers, and breakup bouquets.

I shouldn't be surprised that she's walking in early. She never could resist checking the morning order line up. Even though we both know she memorized it last night. And checked it on her phone probably twenty minutes ago.

"You're off the clock," I call, not looking up. "Go home. Live a little."

"I live here," Willa says, already halfway to the cooler. "Besides, you know I'd panic if I didn't check the dahlias."

"They're fine," I say, pulling out the stack of cards I need to design today. I have several and they need to be sent to the printers before I can take them off my huge to do list.

"They're *never* fine unless I check them myself," Willa shoots back, yanking the door of the cooler open. "Last time, you stored them next to the anemones."

"And?" I glance up, smirking.

She spins on her heel and looks at me like I dropped the biggest scandal. "They *bruised.* They *emotionally* bruised, Eden."

I sigh dramatically and wave my pen in the air like a white flag. "Remind me again which one of us is in need of therapy."

"You," she says sweetly. "Because I self-regulate through micromanagement and martinis."

She starts muttering flower names under her breath like a monk reciting incantations.

I go back to my lettering, but I'm smiling now. She won't say it, but she came early because she knows this week is a landmine. This is the first anniversary of the divorce and the beginning of Valentine's season. I've been extra weird about ink consistency and aggressively labeling drawers.

She's not here to check on the dahlias, she's here to check on me. And she'll pretend otherwise until I'm ready to say it out loud, though. I love her for that.

Even if she *did* reorder all the card stock and rename it "neutral ivory" instead of "bone," just to spite me.

My divorce from Chase was awful—mostly because I genuinely thought we were doing fine. Great, even. I had been planning to talk to him about starting a family.

I made his favorite dinner, lit candles, picked out a bottle of wine we'd been saving. I tried to create the perfect setting for a big conversation. I was nervous, but hopeful. Vulnerable in a way that felt good—like we were moving forward.

But he never came home.

Instead, I was served divorce papers. No explanation. No conversation. Just a doorbell, a manila envelope, and a goodbye I didn't even get to hear in person.

Eventually, I found out why.

He'd been sleeping with my younger sister. For months. Maybe longer.

Evangeline and I were never especially close. We're only thirteen months apart, but it may as well have been thirteen years. She was the influencer, the cheer captain, the girl with the million-watt smile. I was the quiet one—the girl who spent Saturday nights with sketchpads and ink samples, perfecting place cards while she perfected her winged eyeliner.

Looking back, it makes sense. Chase was captain of the football team. She was captain of... everything. They matched in a way we never really did. Glossy, curated, all surface-level shine.

People said he married the wrong sister. They'd even say it to my face. Eva laughed about it once, I could have hit her. My parents disagreed, at least, they always believed he chose right. I was the one who stayed close to home, who called regularly, who sat through awkward dinners and made the effort. Eva only came around when it benefitted her.

Now Chase and Eva are married. Two months after I signed the papers, they had the wedding of their dreams. My parents refused to go. His parents handled everything.

They'd never thought I was good enough for their golden boy anyway.

The worst part? Chase never really loved me. He married me out of spite to win a fucked up competition. To get back at Nash Grady, his best friend at the time. The one who told me he wanted to be with me the night before graduation.

I said no.

Not because I didn't care. I did. But Chase had already painted the picture so perfectly. He made promises I wanted to believe. And Nash... well, Nash was way more mature than his age. He was smart, kind, and always there when I needed him. And I wasn't brave enough for that kind of love yet.

I think about that night more than I should.

Do I wonder what life would've looked like if I'd chosen him? Maybe. Especially on the nights when I'm alone with just a frozen meal and a glass of wine.

But I've made one promise to myself, and I intend to keep it. I won't get involved with anyone who has ties to Chase Whitaker ever again.

"Earth to Eden." Willa waves a hand in front of my face, eyes narrowing.

I blink up at her. She's no longer fussing over the cooler —she's standing right in front of me now, one brow raised like she already knows the answer.

"Let me guess... mind on Chase?"

"Yeah." I sigh, pushing back from the counter. "It's that time of year."

"I get it, E. I do." She softens, then exhales. Here it comes. "But he was never good enough for you. You deserve so much better."

"And I'll get it," I say, trying to sound confident. "Eventually."

"You're young!" she bursts out, tossing her hands in the air.

"And divorced at twenty-five. Not exactly the glow-up arc I was aiming for."

"No," she says, pointing at me like she's issuing a decree. "You're a young woman who got betrayed by a total loser. Big difference."

Right on cue, the front door chimes.

Willa glances up. "Well look who just walked in."

I look up to see that it's Mr. Hal Perkins, our seventy something year old mailman, retired twice and still somehow on the route.

"Ladies," he greets, stepping inside with a stack of envelopes and a smile that creaks like an old screen door. "Y'all got more cards than the courthouse today."

"We're the heartbreak headquarters," I reply, taking the stack from him. "Thanks, Hal."

"You takin' care of yourself?" Willa asks, already moving to grab him a bottle of water from the mini fridge under the counter. "It's freezing out."

Hal waves a hand. "My knees are complaining, but my heart's still good. That counts, right?"

"You're the only man I trust with my heart these days," I say with a grin.

He chuckles. "Don't let your mama hear you say that."

Willa hands him the water, and he tips his hat to both of us. "Y'all behave. And tell those roses of yours to stop tempting the local widows. I got ambushed at the senior center thanks to your Valentine's window display."

Willa beams. "My work here is done."

He leaves, and I flip through the envelopes. Bills,

coupons—nothing interesting. Until I reach a thick black one that makes me pause.

The paper is matte and velvety to the touch, heavier than anything else in the stack. There's no return address, just my name in silver ink across the front. Eden Taylor. Beneath that, my shop. Ink & Stems, 227 Briarwood Lane. No city, no state, no zip code. Like whoever sent it already knew exactly where to find me.

The handwriting is unfamiliar—looping and elegant, just a little too perfect to feel casual. I turn it over, noting the flap sealed with deep red wax. The surface is smooth, with no emblem or initials.

It looks like something meant for a secret society. Or something given to someone after a funeral. Or possibly both.

I break the wax seal carefully, slipping my finger beneath the flap.

Inside is a single black card. Heavy stock. Edges trimmed in deep crimson foil.

The front says *To My Almost Valentine*.

My breath catches. *Almost?*

I open it.

> *Roses are red,*
> *Violets are blue,*
> *Some never left*
> *The same path to you.*
> *The door may be closing,*
> *The path may be crossed,*
> *But what you once wanted*
> *Is never quite lost.*
> *No whisper will name it,*
> *No promise will say,*

But the one you remember
Could be on their way.
Happy Valentine's Day.

Willa sees it too. "That was... ominous."

I turn the card over again to check the envelope for the third time. "There's no name. No return address. Not even a postmark. It's like it just... showed up."

Willa raises a brow. "Creepy poetic secret admirer energy. We love that for you."

I stare at the card, my fingers tightening slightly around the edges. "Except I don't have admirers. Secret or otherwise."

"Maybe it's not about admiration," she says, plucking a tulip from a nearby bucket. "Maybe it's a warning."

"Better," I deadpan. "A Valentine's Day threat. Perfect."

Willa shrugs, completely unfazed. "Or maybe it's just someone trying to be mysterious and missed the landing."

She twirls the tulip like it's a wand. "People do weird stuff this time of year. Love makes them dumb."

I slide the card back into the envelope, still unsettled. "Well, if I get murdered by a masked Valentine, at least make sure the flowers at my funeral aren't red."

"I'd never do you dirty like that," she says, deadly serious. "Strictly whites and greens. Classy. Maybe a hint of blush."

"Good," I mutter, dropping the envelope on the counter like it might bite me. "Because this? Definitely not normal."

Willa's already heading back to the cooler. "Neither is running a flower-slash-calligraphy shop in a town of two hundred, but here we are."

I snort. "Living the dream."

She points a tulip at me like it's a mic. "Say it with me: ominous Valentine or not, we are unbothered."

"Deeply bothered," I mutter, turning the envelope over again.

"Mentally unwell but aesthetically thriving," she calls back.

Fair.

I go through the rest of the pile until I hit a card I really didn't want to see.

Our class reunion.

Because apparently, someone decided that *seven years* was a meaningful milestone. Who does that? Who throws a reunion before the decade mark?

Oh right—our class. The one that threw a graduation after party with custom cocktails. Of course they want another excuse to dress up, drink, and casually brag about their "thriving" lives.

Nothing says nostalgia like a catered ego boost. Some things never really change.

"Willa," I call, already regretting it, "please tell me we're not popular enough to be invited to things."

She peeks around the cooler, wiping her hands on her apron. "Is it another influencer wedding with a ten page dress code?"

"Worse." I flip the envelope over. "Class reunion."

She groans like I just said group project. "Didn't we just have one?"

"No. That was the Alumni Networking Holiday Mixer, remember? Hosted by Tara Quinlan's LinkedIn addiction."

Willa walks over, snatching it from my hand. "Seven years? Who does a reunion at seven years?"

"Our class," I deadpan. "The same people who live for

themed parties and peaked in high school, but are trying to hide it."

She opens the invite like it's going to explode glitter. She was right… it does. The card is matte black with silver lettering. Gothic, formal, entirely too self important.

HOSTED BY: Ms. Valentine
LOCATION: Provided Upon RSVP
DRESS CODE: Masquerade – Masks Required

Willa reads it twice. "Ms. Valentine? That's not a person. That's a Batman villain."

I shake my head. "She's real. Sort of."

Willa's already moving back toward the cooler, tulip in hand. "Oh, I know *of* her. Everyone in the floral scene does. The Valentine's Masquerade is legendary. Exclusive. High drama. And no one actually knows who throws it."

"Exactly," I say, flipping the invite again. "No return address. No first name. Just… Ms. Valentine."

Willa taps the back of the card like it's obvious. "Might as well RSVP. It's a masquerade. No one will know it's us anyway."

"A masquerade," I repeat quietly, considering that

Willa's already turning back toward the cooler. "Worst case? Free champagne and a mask to hide behind."

I tuck the envelope under the counter, next to the receipts and the pen I never lend out.

It's probably nothing.

Just a party.

Just a card.

All this will be fine… right?

13

CHAPTER TWO

Nash

I always feel like I'm lost in the world around me. Everyone in this godforsaken town is full of life while hiding all their shit behind closed doors.

I never accepted that. Probably why I moved away to begin with.

Until my mother begged me to come home, sharing that my childhood crush, Eden Taylor, got divorced. And my shitbag childhood best friend broke her heart when he fucked and married her narcissist of a sister.

No one should be surprised. It's not that I don't feel bad for her. I do. But she made her choice—and it wasn't me. I wanted her, I said so, plain as day. And she looked at me like I'd handed her something she didn't ask for.

Then she walked away. Straight into his arms.

I can't blame her for being scared. But I won't pretend it didn't gut me.

It's been a week since I moved back. Long enough to unpack the boxes but not long enough to pretend I'm staying for good. I keep telling myself it's temporary.

That I'm only here until my mom settles into the house I bought her—the one closer to town.

We used to live in one of those falling apart apartment buildings off Maple Street. Paper thin walls. Mold in the vents. I swore I'd get her out someday.

Now she's got keys to a real place. And I've got no excuse to stick around.

I left this town right after graduation and never looked back. Couldn't watch the girl I loved marry my best friend and pretend it didn't matter. So I got gone, fast. It made it easy on them, if Chase noticed at all. And staying would have killed me. Chase Whitaker. He was my best friend—until he wasn't.

The kind of guy who didn't need to try hard to win. Captain of everything. Voted most likely to charm your mama and steal your girlfriend. He didn't even want Eden. Not really. He just wanted to beat me to her.

I'd told him how I felt. During senior year, late one night, sitting in my truck, I said it straight: I was gonna ask her out. Eden Taylor—the girl I'd been in love with since she handed me a twisty tie ring in fifth grade and said I had to marry her someday.

He smiled like a damn vulture and told me I should.

The next day, he told me she'd asked him out. Said it like it was no big deal. Like he hadn't heard me say I was going to ask her.

I believed him. For a while. It wasn't until later that I found out that wasn't how it went at all. He'd made the first move. And after they got together—he cheated. Constantly.

She never knew. Or maybe she did and just didn't want to see it.

That's when I knew I couldn't stay. It wasn't just about

losing her. It was about realizing the person I'd called my best friend was never really on my side to begin with.

I didn't go to the wedding. I had no idea it was even happening until Willa texted me weeks later like she didn't know how to say it.

"They're married," she said. "It wasn't even big. More like a power move than a love story."

I shoved the phone in a drawer and didn't touch it for a week.

I've stayed gone for almost ten years. Built a life far from here. Told myself I was over it.

Until Willa called again. They got divorced. It was ugly. Turns out he was screwing her sister—Eva. Two months after Eden signed the papers, he married Eva. Like it was some damn game. Not to mention it seems that Evangeline Taylor has always been more his type—full of ego and self indulgent. The complete opposite of Eden.

I didn't even know what to say. So I told her I didn't want to know.

I turn off the main road, dirt kicking up behind the tires of my motorcycle as I ease down the narrow drive. The house comes into view, framed by tall oaks—white siding, fresh paint, a wraparound porch, and window boxes already full of her favorite snapdragons. The porch swing sways like it's waiting for someone to take a seat. The porch light's already on, even though it's barely sunset. That's my mom. Always one step ahead of the dark. You had to be where we lived before.

I kill the engine and swing off, my knees popping in protest as I stretch. Helmet in one hand, I take a breath, staring up at the place.

It's nothing like the apartment we had growing up—two bedrooms above a busted laundromat that always smelled like bleach and mildew. This place has space. Covered in windows. A front yard she keeps trimmed herself. She's proud of it, too—tells everyone she finally got her porch and her peace.

She loves it. It's the first time she's lived somewhere that doesn't feel like it's on borrowed time.

The front door's unlocked like every door on this side of town. Folks here still believe no one's got a reason to steal what's been earned the hard way.

I push it open without knocking.

"Hey, Ma," I call out, dropping my helmet onto the bench by the door.

She's at the stove, stirring something in her favorite chipped Dutch oven. She doesn't turn right away.

"You're late," she says. "And you smell like the road."

I huff a laugh, toe off my boots. "Good to see you too."

My mom's been running our household solo since I was six. Never complained. Not once. She just worked—two jobs, sometimes three. Woke up early, came home late, tied her apron tight, and made whatever we had stretch further than it should've gone. Rent, groceries, gas, school supplies. She always figured it out.

Her name's Sharon but to me, she's just *Ma*. Always has been. She is the kind of woman who can fix a leaky faucet with one hand and hold your whole damn world together with the other. We didn't have much growing up, but she made it feel like enough. Like we were enough.

I don't remember much about my father. The sound of boots on linoleum, the slam of the front door, and Ma not flinching when it happened. He left mad and stayed gone. She never said why. I never pushed. Whatever it was, it didn't matter more than staying on our feet.

She never remarried. When I was old enough to ask, she

always said that one man walking out was enough of a lesson. But she loved me hard. Like it filled in the cracks. And maybe it did.

Now here I am back under her roof. Temporarily, I keep saying. Helping her settle into this new house closer to town. It's the first place she's had that feels like hers. She walks through it barefoot, humming, like she's finally allowed to take up space. Like maybe she's starting over too.

She wouldn't have bought the house on her own. So, I bought it for her. I didn't tell her at first, just had the realtor call with a miracle offer and waited until the keys were in her hand to admit it.

The idea didn't come from nowhere, either. Back when I was drifting, bouncing from town to town, shop to shop, sleeping where my bike stopped, I started putting every spare dime into Wes Burke's idea. He's been my best friend since before we were potty trained. The only person who looked at my mess and didn't flinch. He told me if I gave him two years and a gut-renovated lease, he'd give me something real.

Wes believed in me when I didn't believe in myself. He called me every damn week until I stopped running long enough to listen. He built the dream. I built the bones. Vintage finds, custom pieces, antique restoration—I tracked them all down and brought them home. He made them shine.

Now Burke & Grady Vintage is the kind of place people book a year in advance just to get on the client list. We've been called the best vintage shop in Mississippi. Maybe even the South as a whole. It bought me just enough peace to come back here and hand my mom the kind of life she always gave me, even when she had nothing.

I told her it was stability. But really—it was just the only way I knew to say thank you.

She finally glances over her shoulder, smile tugging at her mouth. "Mm hmm. I've got cornbread in the oven and stew on low, so sit down before you fall down."

I ease into the chair by the kitchen table, stretching out legs that still ache from the ride.

"How was work?" She asks, moving around the kitchen like it's right where she belongs.

"Haven't started yet. I'm still figuring out what comes next."

She hums. It sounds neutral, but I know her well enough to hear the meaning behind it. "You'll land on your feet here," she says. "You always do."

I glance over at her. "Didn't say I was staying."

She doesn't look at me. "No, you didn't," she agrees. "But I know that look you get when you're about to run. I also know the one you get when you don't really want to."

I lean back in the chair, arms crossed. "I told you that this is just until you're settled."

"You think this house needs that much settlin'?" She snorts softly. "Baby, I can hang my curtains and build my shelves just fine. What I can't do is keep pretendin' like this town don't still have pieces of you in it."

That makes me think about things more than I wanted to.

She finally turns to face me, towel in hand, eyes reading everything but kind. "You left runnin'. Fast as you could. I let you because I knew why. But maybe it's time you stop runnin' and see what's still yours if you want it."

I don't answer. Can't yet. So she goes back to her stew like she didn't just drop the truth straight into the middle of the kitchen.

She clicks the spoon on the side of the pot. Then—light as anything—she speaks. "You got mail."

I blink. "What?"

She points toward the counter with her elbow. "Envelope came this morning. Looked important."

Sure enough, it's there. Right by the recipe box, sits a matte black envelope, the paper is heavy and there's no return address.

She doesn't look up. "Figured it wasn't a bill. Not unless the power company got real fancy."

I turn it over. No stamp. No seal. Just weight and ink. Ripping the flap open, and sliding the matte black card out, I read.

HOSTED BY: Ms. Valentine
LOCATION: Provided Upon RSVP
DRESS CODE: Masquerade – Masks Required

I read it twice.

Ma finally turns from the stove, wiping her hands on a dish towel. "Well? What is it?"

I hold the card up like it might explain itself. "Class reunion invite. Masquerade theme."

She squints. "Didn't y'all graduate, what—seven years ago?"

"Yeah." I toss the envelope on the counter. "Apparently, that's long enough to forget how much we all hated each other."

She lets out a short laugh. "Ain't nobody got real jobs or real kids yet. What're y'all reuniting for—trauma bonding?"

I grin, despite myself. "Some of 'em probably wanna flex."

"Mmm." She picks up her spoon again, stirring like she's thinking it over. "Let me guess. Hosted by one of those girls with a blog and a wine brand?"

"Worse. No name. Just 'Ms. Valentine.'"

That gets her attention. "Ms. Valentine?" she repeats, turning back around. "You mean that invite-only thing with the masks? That's real?"

I shrug. "Guess so. Says it's for the reunion too. Double the mystery. Double the awkward."

She raises a brow. "You gonna go?"

I shake my head. "Nah. No point."

Ma gives me a long look, the kind that means she's letting me dig my own grave before she lowers the shovel. "No point, huh?"

"You know how I feel about those people," I say. "A room full of folks pretending they didn't spend four years making each other miserable? Hard pass."

She leans back against the counter, arms crossed. "And what if she's there?"

I freeze. She doesn't have to say the name. We both know exactly who she is talking about.

"I'm not going to crash some weird high school fever dream just to *maybe* stand across the room from Eden Taylor in a mask."

"Mmm," she hums. "Didn't say you had to. Just figured you might want the chance to see if anything's different."

"It's not." I cross to the fridge, needing something cold to justify how hot my neck feels. "She chose Chase."

"She was a kid," Ma says softly. "So were you. The story might not be over."

I crack open a beer. "You always did love her more than me."

"I love y'all exactly the same," she says, smirking while she pulls the pot off the burner. "I just think some things deserve a second look. Even if they still hurt."

I don't say anything.

She sets a bowl in front of me. "You should go."

"I'm not gonna know anybody there," I say. "We're all strangers now."

"That's what the masks are for," she says with a wink. "Be whoever you want for a night."

I sigh, staring down at the bowl. Stew with all the fixins. My favorite. She's playing dirty.

"Fine," I mutter. "But I'm not dancing."

She grins, victorious. "You always say that."

CHAPTER THREE

Eden

I still can't believe I'm doing this. I didn't plan any of it. I actively refused, actually. Said no at least five times. So, Willa took over—handled the outfits, the masks, the RSVPs. Now it's the night of the masquerade, and I'm about to find out what she picked.

"Here we are!" She announces, bursting into my bedroom like she's delivering life changing good news.

I moved in with her after the divorce. Her two bed, two bath apartment is right down the street from the shop. Easy access to town. Living with my best friend after my life fell apart wasn't the worst idea I've ever had.

She's carrying two garment bags like we're about to perform and compete for the most important beauty pageant in the world. She drops them on my bed with a flourish she absolutely practiced in the mirror. I'd be lying if I said her enthusiasm doesn't make me smile despite it all.

She unzips hers first and reveals a midnight blue dress that looks like it was made from starlight. It's backless and fitted, the kind of dress that turns heads and knows exactly why.

"Subtle," I say.

"It's called *power dressing*," Willa replies, holding it against her body. "Midnight mogul meets main character. I'm going full ex-boyfriend's biggest regret tonight."

I snort, because of course she is.

Then she turns to the other one and unzips the bag. "And this," she declares, "is *your* revenge dress. But classy. The kind that ruins a man's evening. Or at least one man in particular."

It's emerald green and strapless, with a deep neckline and a snatched waist that'll make people double take. The fabric looks soft but structured like it means business. Gold thread edges the bodice and hem. Understated, but not forgettable.

I hate to admit that it's totally me.

The mask is a soft gold filigree with a subtle gleam. Pretty without trying.

I blink. "This doesn't scream 'I forgot my ex exists.'"

"It screams I upgraded without speaking," Willa says, arms crossed like she just won something. "Let them wonder who you are. Let them hate how much they care."

I raise an eyebrow. "You mean let them hate how hot you look."

"Try it on," she urges, already kicking me toward the bathroom like a stage mom.

I give her a look. "If I come out looking like the knockoff version of a Greek tragedy, you're fixing it."

"I'd never let you be a knockoff," she says, smug. "You're the main event."

I shut the bathroom door and slip into the dress, half expecting it to betray me in some dramatic, zipper splitting fashion. But it doesn't. It slides on like a satin glove.

When I step out, Willa's already perched on the edge of

the bed, scrolling through something on her phone. She looks up and freezes.

"Well damn," she breathes. "Okay, Greek tragedy. More like goddess."

I laugh, adjusting one strap. "You're ridiculous."

"You're stunning," she counters, standing to adjust the mask in my hands. "You're gonna walk into that masquerade and remind people why Chase lost a good one."

"Pretty sure they whispered my name like some damn punchline."

Willa's expression softens. "Mostly because you left without giving them a show. And now? You're the encore." Her smile brightens even more. "Nash is going to lose his mind."

The look on her face is one of pure terror. Her eyes go wide, her hands fly to cover her mouth, she's speechless. For the first time in her entire life, probably.

I study her face for a beat, then say it before I can stop myself. "You stayed in touch with Nash, didn't you?"

She doesn't flinch. Just sighs. "Yeah. I did."

"Why?"

Willa shrugs, but it's too practiced. "Because someone had to. He didn't ask me to. I just... couldn't not."

"You never told me."

"Because he swore me to secrecy. And you were already drowning in your own problems."

I sit on the edge of the bed, smoothing the fabric of my dress. "Did he ever ask about me?"

Willa is quiet for a moment. "He didn't... but I knew he wanted to."

I swallow the lump in my throat, fingers tightening around the edge of the mask. "He's really back."

She nods, like she's been waiting for me to catch up. "Yeah. He's back."

"Why now?"

Willa sits next to me, hands clasped in her lap like she's trying to be careful with the truth. "His mom's moving. Bought a house closer to town, and he came back to help her get settled."

I nod slowly. Of course. That tracks. That's who he is.

"That's all?" I ask, even though I'm not sure which answer would hurt more.

Willa tilts her head. "That's why he came back. But that's not why he's still here." Willa adjusts one of the straps on my dress, pretending like it needs it. It doesn't. She just needs something to do with her hands.

"You know," she says lightly, "I always thought you should've ended up with him."

I blink at my reflection. "Willa."

"I'm just saying." She steps back, arms crossed, giving me the once over. "Chase made sense on paper. Nash made sense in real life."

"It was high school," I say, but it sounds like a weak excuse even to me. "I didn't know what I wanted."

"You knew," she counters softly. "You were just scared of wanting it."

I meet her eyes in the mirror. There's no judgment there. Only the bone deep knowing only your best friend ever gets to hold over you.

"I never thought that he felt that way about me," I admit. "And then it turns out he did. But he told me right before graduation, and I panicked. Then Chase was... there. Offering forever like it was a sure thing."

"Except it wasn't," Willa says, voice changes to something more gentle now. "It was just words and noise. Nash was different. Kept things to himself. Introverted. That doesn't mean what he said wasn't real."

I swallow, throat tight.

"Maybe this is your chance to find out if you two were ever really meant to be, E." Willa grabs my hand and squeezes. Not back then... now. With a clean slate, and no extra noise."

"Great," I say sarcastically. "A seven year class reunion with my favorite people. Good time to figure all this shit out surrounded by my ex husband, bitch of a sister, and everyone else who always made fun of me. My dream come true."

The ride is exactly twenty seven minutes of me pretending to be calm while slowly dying inside. Willa doesn't help. She puts on Beyoncé like we're going into battle—which, fine, we kind of are—but I'm too busy trying not to sweat through my dress to appreciate the mood.

"This was a mistake," I say for the thousandth time as we pull up to the estate.

"Nope," Willa replies, shifting into park. "This is a statement."

A *statement* that I have absolutely lost my mind.

The house is massive. The kind of Southern mansion people rent out for lifestyle shoots and haunted history tours. Oaks line the drive, limbs like bent arms pointing at me like they're teasing me. There are actual lanterns flickering in the trees, like fireflies dancing in the breeze.

"This looks cursed," I mutter, stepping out in heels I hate to admit I love.

Willa ignores me and fluffs her hair. "This looks expensive."

Same thing.

The entrance is really just two people in black suits standing behind a velvet rope like they've been trained by the CIA. I clutch my envelope like it's a hall pass to hell.

We walk up and I hand mine over. The man—who might actually have actually been trained by the British guards for how much emotion he shows—flips it open, scans the name, then steps aside without a word.

I blink. "That's it?"

Willa shrugs. "You thought it would self destruct or something?"

"I was prepared for fire," I admit. "At least smoke."

We step through the gate, and it's like walking into someone's very rich fever dream. The lawn is glowing with fairy lights and candles in floating bowls. A string quartet is playing something dramatic enough to make me question my life choices. Everyone is masked. Everyone is beautiful. Everyone looks like they know exactly who they are and I am just a woman in emerald satin trying not to pass out.

Willa leans in. "Still want to bail?"

"Every second," I whisper. "But you did good. This dress is kind of magic."

"I know," she smirks. "Now hold your head up. No one here cares about us. Not really. Plus they all peaked in high school anyway."

Willa and I stick to the edge of it all, watching the crowd with matching expressions of half curious, half braced for impact.

We haven't even stepped fully through the archway yet before I spot them.

Chase Whitaker and Evangeline Taylor-Whitaker.

Of course she added the hyphen. Least anyone forget that she's the sister that 'won'

They're standing by the fountain like someone handed them a script and told them they're the leads. Chase is in a gold suit that practically screams 'look at me,' his mask is the same shade. The thing has a crack down one side that somehow makes it look even more self important.

Eva's in white. Not simple white—*blinding* white. Clean lines, dress cut low enough to make a preacher wince, mask stark and smooth like it was meant to show off her perfect makeup.

He is in all gold with white accents. She is in all white with gold accents. They want to be noticed.

They're laughing too loud. They want attention. Actually it is more like they want approval. Chase giving that grin he perfected in high school, the one that always says *I know I'm the prize.* Eva tilts her head, all calm and collected, eyes scanning the crowd like she's already appraising who's inferior.

I know I shouldn't care. I really don't want to care. But as much as I tell myself *they're not worth it...* my chest tightens in this way I've worked so damn hard to pretend I don't remember anymore.

Willa doesn't say anything. She slips her arm through mine, grounding me.

We haven't even gone inside the building yet. And already, I'm remembering just how hard it is to pretend the past doesn't creep up on me.

I turn to the left just a bit and that's when I see him.

Nash Grady.

He's in a black suit that fits too well. The charcoal mask doing nothing to hide the line of his jaw or the way he scans the crowd. I can tell he's already done with it all.

He's still tall. Still has this serious look on his face. And somehow, even across all this time, he's still every inch the boy I almost chose... except now, there's no boy left. Now he's a man who has no interest in reliving the past.

Seven years. One look.

And just like that, I'm rehashing the one choice that screwed everything up when I picked the wrong guy at eighteen.

CHAPTER FOUR

Nash

W ell, shit. They really went all out.

String lights hang like they cost more than sense, the fountains are bubbling like this town has ever had that much grace. People are dressed like they've got something to prove.

Hell, maybe they do. It's not every day a bunch of washed up twenty somethings get to put on masks and pretend they didn't peak at eighteen.

I don't recognize half of these people. Don't want to, either. The ones I *do* recognize, I hope don't recognize me.

They're all laughing, drinking, hugging each other like they're proud to be here. Like they don't see each other at every other function this town holds. Most of them never left town, if they did they didn't go far. There's only a handful of us that ran as soon as possible.

They're acting like nothing ever happened. Like the man in the gold mask didn't fuck over his wife and marry her sister in the most public way possible.

Chase fucking Bennett.

He's working the room already—gold smile, gold drink, gold crack in his mask. Ironically that may be something that shows his true personality.

He and Eva look perfect. On paper anyway. Who knows if their reality is as picture perfect as they portray. I hope it's not.

I watch them walk by a group of women who used to whisper behind Eden's back. Now they're gushing over Eva's dress.

Nobody blinks. Nobody hesitates.

It's like the whole damn town—and half the state of Mississippi—decided that Chase Whitaker was always hers to begin with. Like Eden never wore that ring.

It makes me sick, how easy it is for people to forget. Or maybe they didn't forget. Maybe they just never cared at all.

I scan the crowd again and see two women walking in together.

The one in blue's arm is through the woman's. But the one in green stops me cold, her emerald dress is cut low at the back, captivatingly so.

I take a step forward without meaning to.

I can't see her full face—just the edge of her mask, the tilt of her chin, the way her mouth curves. She's beautiful.

I damn near forgot what that felt like to be kicked in the ribs like this.

Could it be? No, it can't be.

But it is. I know who it is the moment she laughs. When that soft small sound slips out, everything else around me completely drops away.

Eden.

Her hair is darker than I remember, a little shorter, even. But there's no doubt in my mind that it's her. The mouth I've wanted to kiss since fifteen. The hands I never got to hold. The girl I should have fought for.

I am about to walk up to her when I feel a heavy hand on my shoulder. I turn to look at Wes. He doesn't say anything at first, just lifts an eyebrow like he already knows exactly what I'm about to do and thinks I'm an idiot for it.

"You good?" He asks, dry as ever.

I glance back toward her. That green dress. That mask. That laugh. "Does it matter?"

"Nope." He pops the p, shifts his weight. "Still gotta ask."

"She hasn't seen me."

"Uh huh." He draws it out enough to be annoying. "That why you're breathing like you lost a fight?"

I don't respond.

"She looks good," he adds.

"She looks the same."

Wes snorts. "You wish."

I shoot him a look. He shrugs. "You gonna stand here and pine, or do something useful?"

I don't answer.

He leans in a little. Low enough no one else hears. "Don't spook her, man."

"I'm not—"

He cuts me off with a playful look. "Don't *spook* her."

I don't wait another second. I walk straight to her, hoping she won't tell me to go to hell.

When I get close, I ask, "You wanna dance, or should I stand here lookin' pitiful a little longer?"

She stares at me for half a second, then says, flat as ever, "It's been seven years and that's your opening line?"

I shrug. "Could've gone with a poem. Figured you'd hate that more."

Her mouth twitches. "Nash."

I nod. "Eden."

Willa coughs, loudly. "Are we saying names like idiots or is one of you gonna actually dance?"

Eden shoots her a look. "Do you *mind*?"

"Absolutely not," Willa says, already stepping back. "This is exactly what I came for."

Eden turns back to me, eyes narrowing behind the mask. "If you step on my toes, I'm walking away."

"I'll aim for grace," I say, holding out my hand. "But no promises."

She takes my hand, her fingers curl around mine. I'll take whatever scrap I can get.

I lead her toward the dance floor. People are clearing out space for the next song, couples pairing off. But the moment her palm settles against my shoulder, the rest of the room fades.

I place my hand at her waist. Her other hand hovers at my chest for a second before she sets it there.

We start to sway.

It's not graceful. Not at first. It's like I've been transported back to high school and I'm awkwardly dancing with her at prom.

Her eyes stay down for the first few bars of the song. Watching her feet. Watching mine. Then finally, she looks up.

I meet her gaze.

"I don't hate you," I say quietly.

Her brow lifts. "You think I thought you did?"

"I figured you might've. How I left and everything."

She studies me for a second, then says evenly, "I married your best friend."

"He wasn't my best friend."

She nods, but doesn't say anything. She knows he's never been a friend to anyone other than himself in his life.

We turn slow, the floor moving beneath us. Her body stays stiff for a moment longer—then softens, like her shoulders finally give in to the fact that I'm here, and I'm real.

"You'll be gone again soon," she says, voice catching around the seems. She's not asking. Seems like she's already made peace with it.

I shake my head. "I don't know."

She tilts her head slightly, frowning. "No?"

"I kinda like being home," I say.

That makes her blink. Her hand tightens slightly at my shoulder, fingers curling in before she catches herself. She backs her chest away from me.

Her voice softens. "What've you been doing?"

I let out a breath through my nose, looking down at her. "Traveled. Picked up work wherever I could find it. Mostly garages, custom shops. Learned every inch of a bike, every bolt that keeps it alive. Built a couple things worth keeping. Wrecked a few, too."

She nods, silent encouragement.

"Wes and I started restoring vintage builds a few years back. Full custom work. He handles the engines. I find the builds. Doesn't leave a lot of time for bullshit."

Her lips twitch. "I know."

I blink. "You know?"

"I did your business branding."

My jaw goes slack. "Seriously?"

She shrugs like it's nothing, but I feel it. "Willa talked to Wes. She handed it to me without telling you. You needed signage. I had a pen. Seemed simple at the time."

A low laugh escapes me. I'm a little stunned. "I knew that lettering looked familiar."

Eden smirks. "I figured you wouldn't notice."

"Eden," I murmur, voice roughening, "I notice everything."

Her breath catches—barely. "Why'd you really come back?"

The question doesn't surprise me. The way she asks it, on the other hand, does. It feels like she actually cares.

I don't answer right away. Just sway with her, slow and steady, until the music starts to dip.

"I owed my mama everything," I say finally. "One of 'em was showing up to help her move into a new house."

Eden nods, the smallest motion. "Then why did you stay?"

I open my mouth to answer, but someone taps my shoulder.

Smile like a politician. Mask gold and cracked. Eva on his arm, porcelain mask, perfect teeth, fake sympathy in her eyes.

"Mind if I cut in?" Chase asks.

Eden freezes. My hand stays at her waist.

I look at Chase. He nods like we're old friends, pretending that nothing happened. The asshole.

"Man," he says, reaching out like he might clap me on the back once again. "I haven't seen you in—what's it been —six, seven years?"

"Seven," I say flatly.

"Damn. You look good, brother."

I don't move. Don't give him the room to close the distance. "Now's not a good time," I say.

Chase's smile flickers. "C'mon, it's a dance. It's Eden. You know how we used to—"

"I said no."

He blinks like he didn't hear it right. Eva shifts beside him, clutching his arm like she's playing supportive wife, but her eyes are locked on Eden. She's getting twitchy.

I glance at Eden. She still hasn't spoken. But her fingers are tighter against my shoulder now. Holding on.

My eyes go back to Chase's. "I think you've had your turn."

He looks like he wants to say more—like he's gearing up for some charming as hell retort that'll make it all feel like a joke again—but something in my face must shut that down.

He lifts his hands, grinning like this is beneath him. "Alright, alright. No harm done."

He turns, Eva trailing behind, whispering something that sounds like a start to an argument as they disappear into the crowd.

The second they're gone, Eden steps back. Her hand leaves my shoulder. I turn to her. "Hey—"

"I didn't need you to stand up for me," she says, voice tight.

I raise my hands in surrender. "I didn't mean—"

"I know exactly what you meant." Her eyes flash. "And I don't need it."

Then she's gone before I can utter another word. I don't move.

Eden's already gone—green dress disappearing through the crowd, spine straight but not proud. Bracing for the next thing that'll hurt.

I stay where she left me with my palms open and chest hollow.

"Hell of a reunion," Wes mutters, stepping up beside me.

Willa's not far behind. Her eyes are locked on me like she knows exactly what just happened and that it was all my fault. Her arms are crossed, her mouth a tight line, and if she could throw daggers with her eyes, I'd be a deadman.

"She mad?" Wes asks.

"She's not mad, Wes," Willa snaps. "She's gutted. You just saw the part she let you see."

Wes stiffens beside me, but she doesn't look at him. Her eyes stay locked on me.

"She told me I didn't need to defend her," I say quietly. "When I was just trying to make the asshole go away."

"Because every time she needed defending before, it cost her something she didn't get back," Willa says.

I stare at her.

"She's not weak, Nash. Don't twist it. But Chase..." Willa's jaw tightens. "He didn't just cheat. He hollowed her out."

I feel something coil in my gut. Wes glances at her, but stays silent.

"You ever wonder why she said yes to him instead of you?"

I don't answer.

"She didn't," Willa says. "Not really. She liked you first. She always liked you. But you waited too long. And when Chase showed up wanting her loudly with all of his declaration and flare, she mistook it for love. She said yes because it felt like being wanted. Really wanted. For the first time in her life, she wasn't being compared to Evangeline in any way."

I'm caught off guard. I didn't think that she ever wanted to be with me. That I would have just been her second choice.

"She thought you didn't see her," Willa goes on. "By

the time she realized Chase only saw himself? She'd already said I do in front of half this damn town."

Her voice lowers.

"He didn't just cheat, Nash. He fucked with her head. Made her question every good thing about herself, then called it love. Complimented her in public, cut her down in private, and when she started breaking? He blamed her for it. Said she was too much. Too quiet. Too introverted. Not exciting enough. And then—*then*—he left her for her own goddamn sister and let the whole town call it fate. Like it was some kind of love story and not a four year hit job on the best fucking person I know."

I can't breathe right.

Willa keeps going. "She doesn't fight, Nash. She flees. Because fighting's never saved her. It only got her blamed."

Wes lets out a breath. "Jesus."

"She was twenty three when it ended," Willa snaps. "And no matter who stood up for her, it never mattered since everyone else basically thanked her for letting him go find true love. So don't be surprised if she flinched the second you spoke up."

I swallow hard.

Willa steps closer. "She regretted saying no to you the second the ring was on her finger. I know because I'm the one who held her while she cried on the bathroom floor. Night after night. First year of that marriage, she barely spoke above a whisper. He'd trained her not to."

I can't speak.

"She doesn't need you to fix it," Willa says, stepping in close, eyes hard. "But if you want a place in her life now? You better be ready to stand the fuck still while she crawls her way out of the shit he buried her in and don't you dare flinch when it's ugly."

Willa pulls back. Her eyes linger one more second before she turns.

I'm left standing there with Wes, the two of us steeped in the kind of bullshit that reminds me exactly why I left this shithole town to begin with.

CHAPTER FIVE

Eden

My mind won't shut up. Every thought's too loud, moving too fast. I'm drowning in the chaos.

I know I shouldn't have snapped at Nash. I know he meant well. But the second he stepped in, I felt it—that pull in my chest, like I was losing control of my own life all over again.

I hate when people try to stand up for me. It makes me feel small. Poor little helpless Eden. I can't stand it. Especially tonight of all nights.

I need to get the fuck out of here before I do something stupid. What I want to do is punch my asshole ex-husband, or maybe rip my sister's god awful extensions out of her thin hair.

But neither of those things would help the situation, they'd make it so much worse.

"Eden!" Willa's voice cuts through the pulse of the music. She grabs my arm just as I reach the edge of the ballroom.

"Don't," I mutter. "Please. I can't—"

"I know," she says. Her grip tightens slightly to help ground me. "But you can't bolt either. Not yet."

The room's filling fast. We were a small class, sure—but everyone brought someone. Spouses, hookups, handsy old flings. All of them dressed to impress.

I glance back toward the dance floor. Nash is still standing there along with Wes. He's barely holding it together. I know that he is doing everything he can to not run after me. Or maybe he wants to hit Chase as much as I do.

And there's that asshole—already laughing again like none of it touched him.

My jaw tightens. Before I can move, Willa steps in front of me. "Breathe," she says. "Two more minutes. Then we slip out the side, no drama."

"Two minutes is too long," I say, already turning.

Willa doesn't stop me. She walks me to the front door but is staring longingly. I would never ask her to leave. "You stay. I'm fine. I'm just going to spend the night at my parent's house."

At the edge of the corridor, she pauses. "You sure?"

I nod. "If I stay, I'm gonna say something I can't take back. That doesn't mean you shouldn't have fun."

Willa sighs, then scans the ballroom one more time like she's mentally cataloging everyone she'd gladly set on fire.

"Text me when you get to your parents'," she says, clearly worried about me.

"I will," I promise, hoping I remember to do so. She's the type that will show up if I wait too long.

"And Eden?"

I glance back.

Her voice drops. "Don't let them pull you under again. You already crawled out once. You made it."

I swallow hard. "I know."

She reaches out, squeezes my hand once, then lets go. "Go."

I slip through the door and into the cold.

Alone. It's exactly what I need right now.By the time I reach my car, my hands are shaking. It doesn't matter. I slide in, and start the engine.

I don't turn on the radio. I don't even check my phone. I just drive, letting the road guide me down the familiar route.

The roads stretch long and flat past old farmland and sagging fence lines. A few porch lights glow like lighthouses in the dark.

There are no headlights behind me, no signs of the life I just slipped out of. Just a two lane blacktop and the soft hum of my tires on asphalt.

Fifteen minutes out, the edge of town gives way to pastures and scattered oak trees. The sky's bigger out here.

By the time I see the porch light, I'm even more glad that I drove to the reunion.

The house is my safe haven. My comfort place. White siding, chipped in the same corner it's been since high school. Porch steps wide, worn in the middle. Tin roof overhead that is still loud as hell when it rains.

I may live close, but I need my parents. And maybe some time to think.

The swing moves once in the breeze.

And the wreath—God, the wreath. The one that my mother insists needs to be left up year round. Bare branches, dried roses, that same old ribbon my mom refuses to replace. It's frayed to shit but still loved with every bit of her.

Eden: Made it to their house.

I put my phone away. She probably won't respond anyway. I hope she's having fun.

I kill the engine but stay behind the wheel for another minute. It's stupid to be nervous. But for whatever reason, I am.

I open the door, my heels clicking against the newly paved driveway. This is an uncharacteristically cold life. Irony of all ironies.

By the time I get to the top step, the front door's already opening.

My mom stands there in her robe—blue plaid, sleeves pushed up, hair pinned in one of those soft claw clips she wears when she's half asleep but still worrying. Hair dark, like mine, but streaked with gray now.

She takes one look at me and steps aside.

My dad's behind her. Still in his work shirt—faded green with his name stitched above the pocket. He never changes into pajamas until the exact moment he's ready to crawl into bed. His hair's gone mostly silver, buzzed short. His eyes don't miss much—same dark set as mine, just lighter along the edges. Eva has my mother's eyes. He doesn't say anything. He already knows how bad it was.

I walk in and once the lock clicks behind me, I break.

I don't mean to cry. Hell, I haven't let a single tear fall in months. But my mom wraps her arms around me like I'm still seventeen and the world just crashed into me, and that's all it takes. My knees don't give, but they try. She smells like chamomile lotion and dryer sheets. I breathe her in like I've been holding it since the dance floor.

"I'm okay," I manage, voice wrecked.

"I know," she says softly. "But you're home anyway."

She pulls back, brushing my hair behind my ear like she used to.

"Tea?" she asks.

I nod. "Yeah. Please."

We move into the living room. My dad sinks into his usual chair, legs stretched out, arms crossed still quiet. My mom disappears into the kitchen and comes back with two mugs, handing one to me. It's my favorite.

We sit, the couch cushions groan beneath us.

"Chase was there," I say. "I knew he would be but still... sucks to see him happy."

My dad shifts, face going still. My mom stiffens beside me.

"With Eva," I add. "He acted like none of it ever happened. Like I was the one being dramatic."

My mom's mouth pulls tight. "He's not welcome here. Hasn't been for a while now."

"He never will be again," my dad mutters. "You know that, right?"

I nod and sigh before blowing on the tea. Then, without really meaning to I say, "Nash was there too."

My mom's eyes flick over to me. My dad straightens, just slightly. Without looking at them, I know they're communicating in the way that only two people who have been together forever can.

"He asked me to dance," I say, quieter. "I said yes."

"Well," my mom says, sipping her tea, "you always did make better choices when he was around."

My dad lets out a breath. "That boy loved you. Always did."

I run a finger around the rim of my mug. "Maybe in high school. But too much time has passed now and too many people have gotten in the way. A lot can happen in seven years. I know that better than anyone."

Neither of them says a word.

"I thought I was doing the right thing back then," I say quietly. "He made it look like love was certainty—no doubts, no waiting. He wanted me publicly, loudly, like he couldn't help himself. And after a lifetime of playing it safe, of wondering if I was ever really seen, that felt like enough. Like being chosen meant it had to be love."

"We wanted to tell you," my mom says gently.

I thought they liked Chase. What are they wanting to tell me? What could I have missed... well besides everything.

"We just wanted you to be happy," my dad says as he leans forward to put his elbows on his knees.

I understand why they never told me. It's not like I would have listened anyway.

My chest tightens. "I didn't want to be a mistake."

"You weren't," my mom says firmly. "But he was."

My dad stands, taking his mug with him. "Don't spend too long looking backward, Eden," he says. "It's easy to get stuck there."

When he's gone, my mom looks over at me, a little softer now. "You think it's too late?" She asks.

I know what she's talking about. My relationship with Nash. I shrug. "It feels like it should be."

She reaches over, and brushes my hair behind my ear once again. "Maybe. But love's stubborn. And so are you."

Eventually, my dad comes back in, mug rinsed, hands in his pockets. "You staying the night?" he asks, already knowing the answer.

I nod. "Yeah. If that's okay."

He snorts. "It's your bed."

My mom stands, pressing a kiss to the top of my head.

"There's clean towels in the hall. I'll turn the heat up in your room."

"I'm fine," I say, out of habit as I get up and head to my childhood bedroom.

The door creaks the same way it always has. The light switch still sticks halfway before it flicks on.

And the room hasn't changed at all. It's the same pale four walls, the same corkboard above the desk with the same few things scattered across it. They're reminders of a teenage girl who had it all figured out. Even the old lamp on the nightstand—the one with the crooked shade and chipped base—is still here, still working.

I stand there for a second, throat tight.

It's like walking into a version of myself I outgrew and left behind at the same time.

I sit on the edge of the bed, fingers brushing the quilt. My mom made this one after I got married—stitched with scraps I recognize from old T shirts and curtains. Pieces of home.

I don't bother turning off the lamp. I lay down on the bed and kick off my heels like I'm still eighteen, waiting for a boy to text back.

I stare up at the ceiling and try not to think.

The truck rattles as he kills the engine. Neither of us moves right away. I'm still holding my shoes in one hand like I'm ready to run, even though I've got nowhere to go.

Nash gets out first. He walks around to my side and opens the door like I'm sure his mama taught him to.

"You don't have to—" I start.

"Yeah," he says. "I do."

So I get out. The porch light's on. My parents always leave it for me. Tonight it feels like a spotlight.

We walk in silence. My hand's on the railing when he says it.

"You looked beautiful tonight."

I almost laugh. I'd spent half the night trying not to cry and the other half pretending I didn't notice Chase disappearing with Eva the second pictures were done.

"Sure," I mutter.

He stops behind me. "You shouldn't have had to wait around like that."

I swallow hard. "Wasn't a big deal."

"It was."

I turn halfway toward him, shoes dangling from my fingers. "Why do you care?"

He holds my gaze without blinking. It's like he's trying to tell me something he doesn't want to say out loud.

"You really don't see it, do you?" He asks, sarcastic chuckle coming out of his mouth.

I frown. "See what?"

He exhales, then throws caution to the wind. "That I'm in love with you."

The words land like a sucker punch in the spine. I should say something. I should tell him he's wrong, or that I don't feel the same, or that this doesn't change anything.

But none of that's true.

What's true is... I do feel it, whenever I think enough about it. I feel for him like I do Chase. I just never wanted to have to make the choice.

"You don't have to say that," I whisper. "Just because tonight sucked."

He shakes his head. "I don't say shit I don't mean, Eden."

I want to say something back. I do. But it's like the words get stuck. Lodged somewhere under my ribs.

Chase and I... we are meant to be.

"You're leaving," I say instead. "It doesn't matter."

"It does to me."

I look at the door. I could open it, step inside, and pretend this never happened.

"I'd stay," he says, voice low. "If you asked me to."

But I don't ask him to. Instead, I turn and walk up the steps. I don't say thank you. I don't say goodnight.

I can't deal with all this.

I want to crawl back into that exact second and beg him not to walk away. To tell him fuck Chase and be with him instead. I wasted seven years of my life. I knew Chase was cheating or at least wanted Eva. Everyone knew it, apparently.

Then my mind drifts to the day that Chase proposed.

The music's bad. The punch is worse. Someone's uncle already started a fight near the truck beds. And I'm barefoot on the lawn, sticky with sweat and sugar, wondering how this night's gonna end.

Chase climbs onto the tailgate.

"Y'all!" he yells, raising a bottle over his head. "I need your attention. I've got somethin' to say."

Laughter breaks out. People whistle. The crowd pulls in. And suddenly—he's looking at me.

He jumps down from the truck and walks toward me, slow and smug, like he knows exactly what he's doing. Like he's been planning this all night.

"Eden Taylor," he says, stopping in front of me, loud enough for God and every gossip to hear. "You're the best thing that's ever happened to me."

I go still. My heart does something reckless.

Then he drops to one knee.

Gasps. Screaming. Willa's hand flies to her mouth. Someone's phone is already out, recording. Someone else yells, "Do it, man!"

Chase pulls out a small black box. The ring is perfect. It's a large oval cut diamond on a gold band.

"Let's make this forever," he says. "Marry me."

The world starts to spin. I know it's fast. I know I'm young. But he's looking at me like I'm gold, like I'm the only girl in the whole damn state who matters. It feels like he can't wait one more second to call me his.

"Yes," I say, breathless. "Yes."

The crowd explodes. He picks me up, spins me. The ring's already on my finger before I can catch my breath.

Eva appears at my side. Her eyes don't leave Chase—not for a second.

"Wow," she says, voice smooth. "Big night."

She leans in just enough to brush her cheek against mine, but it's stiff. For the cameras and parents, not for me.

"Congrats," she says, lips barely moving.

Willa hugs me next. Tight. But when I pull back, her eyes are searching. Her smile doesn't quite reach them. I look away before I can read too much into it.

My parents reach us. My mom touches my arm gently. My dad says, "Well, damn. Guess it's official."

They're both smiling. Proud, maybe. In retrospect, they were probably just trying to be. There's something careful in the way they look at me—like they're holding their words for later. They want to be happy for me. But I also know that they're waiting for me to wake up.

But I don't.

I hold tighter to Chase's hand instead.

Because right now, everyone's watching. Right now, I'm the girl who got the ring. And maybe, if I keep smiling big enough... it'll all feel real.

I didn't see it then—not really. I chalked it up to shock, or jealousy, or Eva just being Eva. But now I see how furious she was. Not because she loved me. Because he was hers, and I was wearing the ring. That fake little smile, the way she wouldn't touch me but wouldn't stop looking at him. She already knew. She knew what Chase really wanted. And it wasn't me.

That brings my mind back to the day my husband fucked me over.

"I think we're done."

He doesn't look at me when he says it. Just pours his drink like it's any other night, then sets the glass down.

"I want a divorce."

The room doesn't move. The clock ticks like it doesn't give a shit. The fridge hums.

"What?" I ask, but it doesn't come out right. I taste blood where I bit my tongue.

Chase doesn't sit. Doesn't shift. He leans against the counter, arms loose, too at ease for what he's about to say. He watches me like his mind is already somewhere else.

"Don't make this dramatic, Eden."

I laugh. I laugh harder. Because if I don't, I'll scream. "Dramatic?"

"Come on," he says, running a hand through his hair. "You had to know this was coming."

I stare at him, trying to find the man I married. The man who used to whisper I was everything. The one who picked me in front of a hundred people.

But he's not here. Maybe he never was.

"No," I whisper. "I didn't know. Because I was busy trying to make this work while you were—"

"Fucking your sister?"

I flinch. "I was gonna say working."

I take a step back like he hit me. My hand grabs the edge of the counter.

"How long," I manage. "How long has it been?"

He shrugs. "Since we were eighteen."

I almost vomit. I almost vomit right there on the kitchen floor.

"That's—" I do the math. "That's our entire marriage."

"Yeah," he says. No guilt. No shame. "I mean, I gave it a shot. Thought maybe you'd grow into the version I wanted. But Eva didn't have to grow. She already is the exact person I want. My perfect match."

"The version—" I choke. "You wanted?"

"You were just... so easy, Eden. Always needing someone to tell you how perfect you were. And Nash? He never would've broken your heart."

My stomach twists. "Nash?"

He grins. Like he's proud of what comes next.

"You really don't know about this, do you?" he says. "Fifteen years old, back porch of Wes' house. Nash tells me he's gonna ask you out. Says he's been in love with you since sixth grade."

I go still.

"And you think I was gonna let that happen?" He laughs. Laughs. "Golden boy gets the dream girl? Not a fucking chance. I'm the top of the food chain. Not him."

My voice is barely a breath. "You married me... to beat him."

"I took you," he says, eyes clear now. "And every time I fucked Eva, I won again."

I can't feel my legs.

"You're a monster," I whisper.

He tilts his head. "Nah. I'm just not pretending anymore. I spent years playing the doting husband while counting down the days until I could stop faking it. You weren't hard to fool—you wanted the dream too bad to look close."

The memory breaks apart like a dish dropped in the sink.

I'm on my back, staring at the ceiling, throat tight, pillow damp beneath me. My whole body's locked up. I can still hear his voice, still see the kitchen, still feel the crack in everything I thought was mine.

I curl onto my side, pull the blanket to my chin, and let the night swallow me whole.

Sleep comes in fragments. Hot, restless. Full of things I never wanted to relive again and the face of a boy I never stopped wanting.

CHAPTER SIX

Eden

I wake up stiff, still in yesterday's dress, makeup smeared and mouth dry. My shoulder's sore from how I curled up, too small for this bed that used to feel bigger.

The ceiling fan clicks overhead. I know *exactly* where I am.

Home.

Or the version of it that still has my high school trophies on a shelf and a dried up corsage in a shoebox under the bed.

Something sizzles in the kitchen. Eggs, probably. Maybe bacon. My mom always cooks too much when she doesn't know what else to do.

I reach for my phone. One message.

Willa: you alive? or do i need to show up with a home-made molotov cocktail?

I snort. Straight and to the point. Very Willa.

Eden: alive. Staying here for a bit then coming back to the apartment.

I don't wait for her to reply. I set the phone down and

swing my legs off the bed, mascara smeared, dress wrinkled, mouth dry.

I'm so glad I came.

The stairs creak under my feet, but I don't bother being quiet. Everyone is up anyway.

My dad's reading something at the table. Paper, not a screen, because he still insists the digital version leaves things out.

Neither of them says anything when I walk in.

My mom just gestures with the spatula. "Sit yourself down, baby. You look like the morning after a storm."

"Thanks," I mutter, dropping into a chair.

She sets the mug down, black as night then slides the cream and sugar over without a word. I fix it the way I like it.

The front door opens without a knock.

The sound of the door creaking open makes my stomach drop. I already know who it is.

"Wow," Eva says from the hallway, voice already high and shiny with attitude. "So this is the walk of shame that finally beat mine. Impressive, Eden. Really impressive."

She floats into the kitchen in a matching set and a fake tan thick enough to stain anything she touches. Sunglasses still on indoors. A walking influencer apology video waiting to happen.

She is orange. How does she think that this is a good look?

"Didn't think you'd still be here," she says. "Thought you'd be long gone after last night. Embarrassing if you ask me. Nash Grady having to stand up for you since you have no backbone and are stuck in the past."

I don't answer. Just take another sip of coffee.

"Eva," my mom snaps without turning around.

"What?" She asks, annoyed by being confronted.

"You can leave."

Eva scoffs, rolling her eyes. "Oh, come on. You're seriously still on this?"

My dad folds the paper and stands. "Give me the key."

Eva blinks. "What?"

"The spare. To this house. You don't get to have it anymore."

"You're kicking me out?" Her voice pitches up. "You're taking *her* side?"

My mom doesn't blink. "You drew the line, Eva. We're just standing where you left us."

"You didn't even come to my wedding!" Eva spits.

"Correct," my dad replies. "We weren't interested in watching our daughter marry her sister's husband."

Eva flushes red beneath her fake tan. "He wasn't her husband anymore."

"He broke her," my mom snaps. "And you threw a party to celebrate it."

"This is insane," Eva says, throwing her arms up. "I'm your daughter, too."

"Then act like the girl we raised," my dad growls.

Eva's hands shake as she reaches into her bag and yanks out the spare key. She slams it on the counter.

"You can act like the victim all you want, but deep down, you knew he'd never stay. He needed more than your sad little life." She laughs in my face. "I didn't fuck with your marriage. You wouldn't give him what he wanted, I did. I'm the one who benefitted."

"Get out," my mom says, voice deadly calm.

Eva stares like she can't believe it. She feels the whole world should've bent over backward to excuse her.

Her mouth opens again, but whatever comeback she

had dies on her tongue. She scoffs. It's loud and fake. "Y'all are unbelievable."

Then she grabs her stupid purse—some ugly mono-grammed nonsense—and storms out in a flurry of perfume and entitlement.

No goodbye. No apology. No looking back.

The front door slams, and the nothing that follows is thunderous.

My mom finally breathes, long and tight, like she's been bracing for impact since Eva showed up.

My dad drags a hand down his face, mutters something under his breath, and sinks back into his chair. I know that he is tired of all this bullshit.

And then mom says what I don't want to hear. "You gonna let her be right?"

It takes me a second to find my voice. "What?"

"You heard her, Eden," my mom says, turning back to the stove. "She thinks you're weak. Thinks you'll never fight for yourself. And you keep letting her."

"That's not fair." I spit it out it too fast, like it'll make it more true.

"No," she says, eyes flashing. "It's true."

My dad doesn't argue.

"You let people walk all over you, baby," he says quietly. "You always have. You give them too much grace, too many chances, and they take and take and take."

"And then you apologize," my mom finishes. "For their selfishness."

I don't know what to say.

"I watched that man dim your light for years," she continues. "When he left, you didn't scream or slam a door. You cleaned up the mess in your life like it was your fault it was broken."

Tears sting, but I blink them back.

"I didn't want to make it worse," I whisper.

"It was already worse," she snaps. "You were drowning, Eden. You smiled through it. Through everything."

My dad leans forward. "You want to be okay? You want to be strong? Then stop flinching every time someone throws a stone. Stand up. Let them know you're still fighting for you."

I nod slowly, but it's not enough for my mom.

"No more hiding," my mom says. "You don't have to be loud. But you do have to show up. For yourself. No one else is gonna do it."

I sit with that. I say the part that's on my mind, that I've never said out loud. "She's still your daughter," I whisper. "I wouldn't blame you if you wanted to keep a relationship with her. I know I'm not always—"

My mom cuts me off fast. "Stop. Don't you dare go down that road."

"She's our daughter," my dad says. "But being family doesn't excuse betrayal. What she did wasn't an accident. She made a choice again and again."

"We didn't go to that wedding because it wasn't a celebration," my mom adds. "It was a spectacle. One meant to humiliate you. We weren't about to sit there smiling while they drove the knife in deeper."

"She didn't even flinch when we told her it was wrong," my dad says. "She laughed. Called us betrayers. As if she hadn't turned her sister's pain into a photo op. Toxicity can be cut out."

"She burned the bridge," my mom finishes. "We just refused to follow her and lose our other daughter."

I stare at the table, my coffee cold and untouched.

"I keep wondering if I was the one who wasn't

enough," I say, voice thin. "That maybe I was too easy to leave."

"You weren't too easy to leave," my dad says. "You were too easy to *use*. That's not the same thing."

It's true. Every part of me that tried to bend, to smooth things over, to keep the peace—I thought that made me strong. The kind of person worth staying for.

All it did was make me convenient.

"You've got fight in you, Eden. Always have. You just never thought you were allowed to use it."

"She made you feel like you had to earn what you already deserved," my dad adds. "That boy... he fed off that. Made your obedience his permission."

"I don't want to be that girl anymore." The words scrape coming out, but I mean them.

"You're not," my mom says.

"You left," my dad adds. "Now it's time you decide where you're going next."

I grab my keys off the hook by the door. My coat. My bag.

At the doorway, I pause. My mom's still by the stove, arms folded now, eyes on me like she's trying to memorize something. My dad meets my gaze and waits. They look at me like they did when I was eighteen. Not the pity I saw before.

"Thanks," I say, choking back my tears. "For not letting me forget who I am."

My mom's voice softens, but her eyes stay locked on mine. "You don't owe us anything, baby. But you do owe yourself the truth."

I let out a breath. "I don't have it all figured out," I say. "But I'm done pretending I'm fine."

My dad nods. "You come back if you need to. But don't stay stuck."

I take a breath. It's shaky, but it won't be for long.

"I won't," I say. "Not this time. I'm done fading into the background. I'm done letting someone else live my life. It's my turn."

I step outside. The cold hits my skin, but it doesn't rattle me. Not this time.

I climb into the car, start the engine, and pull out of the driveway slowly.

Back toward the apartment I share with my best friend.

Back toward my life.

Wherever the hell that's going next, I can't wait to find out.

CHAPTER SEVEN

Nash

I've been at the shop since a little after seven.

Wes is already out on the floor, barking instructions with a wrench in his hand. Music's playing loudly through the speakers, Johnny Cash is everyone's favorite here. Wes always calls it *motivation*.

The guys are welding on the Triumph, sparks are flying everywhere. Tasha's in the front, already wrangling invoices and dragging the new parts inventory into some kind of order.

This office used to be a catch all for crap he didn't want to deal with. Wes finally cleared it out last month and tossed me the keys. He said if I was sticking around, I might as well have a door to close when shit got loud.

It's nothing special—just a desk, a busted fan, and a window that lets me keep an eye on the floor.

Wes dumped everything in the other office. Let's just say desks aren't really his thing.

I spend most of the morning sorting through parts orders and last month's invoices. Wes can rebuild a bike blindfolded, but he couldn't file a receipt if you stapled it to his forehead.

I see what a build could be. He makes it happen.

I shoot off a few emails, call a guy in Baton Rouge about a rare gearbox, and flag a client payment that never hit our account.

Tasha pops in around ten with two coffees and a stack of receipts. She's got paint on her sleeve, attitude in her step, and the kind of precision that keeps this place from falling apart. Tasha's the one who makes everything Wes builds shine.

"You want to yell at the printer or should I?"

I grunt. "I already threatened it. Didn't work."

She smirks, and sets the receipts on my desk. "You're a menace."

When she's gone, I get back to work. Cross checking builds against deadlines. Scheduling freight pickups. Reviewing new custom requests.

By lunch, I'm about ready to crawl out of my own skin.

Wes kicks open the office door with his boot, already grinning. "We're gettin' food before Tasha starts gnawing on brake pads."

Tasha follows, ponytail a mess, smudged grease on her cheek, waving a receipt at me like some kind of white flag. "I haven't eaten since sunrise and someone"—she jerks a thumb at Wes—"stole my protein bar."

"You left it on *my* toolbox," he says.

"Because you think drawers are a conspiracy."

She turns to me. "Come on, Nash. Be the only adult."

I lean back in my chair, and stretch, cracking my back. "Think I'm gonna call it early."

Wes squints. "Everything alright?"

"Yeah." I close the folder in front of me. "Thought I'd drive around. Start looking for a place."

Tasha crosses her arms. "You sure you're not just gonna go park outside Ink & Stems again?"

I give her my best *mind your business* look. "I've never planned on doing that."

"You didn't *have* to," she says smugly.

Wes laughs, already heading out. "Don't do anything dumb."

"Can't make any promises," I mutter.

They're still laughing when they head out, bickering like always.

I take my time cleaning up. Closing the books, locking the drawers Wes never uses. Finally, I kill the lights, slide into my truck, and start to drive.

Ten minutes later, I'm parked across from Ink & Stem. Engine off. Elbows on the wheel. Staring like an idiot.

Watching her shop window like a fool. Like I'm seventeen again, trying to work up the guts to say something real. Half of me wants to walk in and buy something I don't need. The other half knows that'd be worse.

I don't know what the hell I'm doing.

I flinch hard enough to hit my head on the damn roof when the passenger door opens. Willa slides in like it's her truck and not mine, hair a mess, iced coffee in hand. She shuts the door with a snap and looks straight ahead.

"Jesus," I mutter, hand over my chest. "You trying to get yourself punched?"

She sips her drink. "You make it too easy, Grady."

"You stalking me now?" I ask, turning my head back to the shop.

"Nope. Just heading back from a delivery when I saw a

sad looking man staring longingly at a flower shop from the world's least subtle truck."

I shake my head, but she keeps going.

"So. You gonna sit here all day like a Lifetime movie ex husband, or are you gonna do something?"

"Didn't realize this was your business."

"It's Eden's," she says, matter-of-fact. "Which makes it mine. Try to keep up."

I glance over. She's already kicked her boots up on the dash. "It's been three days since the masquerade, Nash."

I don't answer.

She lifts her brows. "What's the game plan here? Sit outside and hope she sends a carrier pigeon?"

"I'm thinking," I mutter, eyes still on the windshield.

"You're stewing," Willa says, crossing her arms. "There's a difference."

I sigh and drag a hand down my face. "She told me to back off."

"She told you not to speak for her. That's not the same thing." She flings back into my face.

I grip the wheel tighter. "She's been through enough."

"Exactly," Willa says. "So stop making her guess what your feelings are. Grow a pair and tell her."

I exhale. "You wanna talk about you and Wes?"

Her mouth twitches and not in amusement this time. "Nope."

"Didn't think so."

She stares ahead, jaw tight, then opens the door. "Figure your shit out, Grady. Before she figures it out for you. This is your second chance. Don't blow it."

She hops out and slams the door behind her.

I sit there for a while after she's gone. Her words still echoing. *Figure your shit out, Grady.*

She's not wrong.

Three days of driving past Ink & Stem. Three days of pretending I'm not waiting for something to change on its own.

I think about Eden, about the look on her face when she walked away. The look that will haunt my dreams for eternity.

The strong and powerful woman I knew withered away to nothing. We can all thank Chase for that.

With no other ideas, I do the one thing I can control. I pull out my phone and I make a call that is about to change my life for better or for worse.

I meet the agent at noon. Missy Ray is blonde to the roots, loud in leopard print, and chewing pink gum as she blows large bubbles. She's got French tips, lashes for days, and a laugh that could peel paint off the walls. Her red Lexus with rhinestone seat covers and a license plate that says *MISS-RAY1* smells like vanilla body spray and hair salon fumes.

She calls me *sugar* before she even asks my name.

Flirty as hell, she talks more about her ex husband than the square footage. Every house we tour, she manages to lean on a doorframe and sigh about how "this would've been perfect if I hadn't caught Ricky with my cousin in a hot tub."

The first house she shows me is a cookie cutter ranch with a red door and all the charm of a hotel lobby.

"Now this is modern *and* move in ready," she says, fluttering her lashes. "Quartz counters, open concept, and the *cutest* little wine fridge. You *do* like wine, right, sugar?"

I grunt.

The second one's worse. Three stories, white brick,

black trim, with so much glass it feels like a fishbowl. Complete with built-ins for a life I don't have, a pool I'd never use, and a bathroom bigger than the shop's office.

"Now this screams *successful bachelor*," Missy Ray croons, popping her gum. "Picture all of it. You, a date, some mood lighting, a bottle of—"

"I'm good," I cut in. "This isn't me."

She pouts. Actually pouts. "You're hard to shop for, Nash Grady."

"Because I'm not shopping for a fantasy," I mutter.

By the third, I'm about ready to call it. Tell her I'll figure it out on my own.

Then I pull up to a place on the edge of town that is set back off the road, hidden behind a line of pecan trees and an old rusted mailbox leaning left.

The dirt drive kicks up a cloud as Missy Ray's Lexus crawls in behind me, her nose already wrinkling, clearly offended by the place's very existence.

She teeters up the drive, heels sinking into the dirt with every step. She nearly face plants trying to keep up with her purse and her pride.

"Oh, honey. *This* one?" she drawls, dragging the word out as if the place personally insulted her. "This is a project."

Exactly. This is the house *I* wanted to see. Not the one she recommended.

The house is old, no denying that—two stories with a wide, sagging porch and a swing hanging by one good chain. The paint's peeling, roof's got a lean, windows older than me and rattling in the frame, but the bones of it are solid.

The lot itself is huge. No neighbors close enough to hear a fight or a laugh.

The porch creaks under my boots. I don't care. The door sticks when I push it open. Still don't care.

More space than I need now.

But maybe not always.

Inside smells like dust and cedar. The floors are worn smooth in places, creaked in others—paths carved by years of the same feet walking the same way. Someone raised a family here. You can feel it.

There's a fireplace with a cracked brick mantle. This time the built-in shelves don't offend me. The sun's caught in the dust, lighting up the faded outlines where picture frames once sat. A life lived here. One that mattered.

Missy Ray clicks around in her heels, nose wrinkled. "It's got an open floor plan and someone added a kitchen island, sure. But no central air, original windows, outdated everything. This place needs a full overhaul." She flicks a crumb off the counter like it personally offended her. "An older couple lived here forever. When they passed, their kids didn't want to deal with it. It's been sittin' for sale for a long time, sugar."

I run my hand along the counter—thick oak, hand carved edges worn smooth. This is the kind of work someone does that is built to last. It was built with love.

"Nah," I say. "An overhaul will take away everything that I love about this place."

She blinks. "You're serious?"

Dead serious.

She launches into a list of issues—foundation cracks, outdated wiring, the way the second floor bathroom is practically a museum exhibit.

But I don't listen to a single thing she says.

I'm already picturing where a new workbench could go in the back shed. Which wall could take a row of framed photos. What it'd be like to hear someone laugh in the kitchen while I come home.

Not any someone.

Eden. I want Eden to be that someone.

"Make the offer," I say, cutting her off mid sentence.

She gapes. "You're joking."

I look around one last time. Yeah. This is the one.

"Nope," I say, turning to Missy Ray. "You can stop showing me places now. This is the one."

CHAPTER EIGHT

Eden

The shop's full throttle.

We're a week and a day out from Valentine's Day, and Willa's buried. So am I.

Two weddings this weekend. Full service. Bouquets, centerpieces, boutonnières, venue installs. All of it.

That's our thing. We don't half-ass love stories.

We handle every detail. Together.

Willa handles the flowers—day of setup, big arrangements, her usual brand of floral magic.

I take the paper. Every place card, every menu, every chalkboard welcome sign that'll end up in someone's wedding album for the next twenty years. I help her on the day of when she needs it.

We make it work. We always have.

And while we're at it, we've got more than twenty Valentine's orders booked, and the phone won't shut up.

It's chaos. Beautiful, blooming chaos.

Willa barrels past me with three bouquets hooked over one arm and a coil of twine swinging from her wrist. "You're doing that thing again."

I don't look up. "If you mean working, then yes."

"No. I mean clenching your jaw like you're trying not to bite someone."

"I'm focused."

She drops the bouquets on the counter next to me, petals brushing my elbow. "Focused people don't look like they're planning a felony."

"That's rude."

"It's accurate," she says, already pivoting toward the register as the bell chimes. She rings up a walk-in—some guy who smells nervous and keeps saying *she likes pink, I think*—then slides back over, snatching the clipboard off the wall.

"Okay. Jameson order's loaded. If I don't leave now, I'm gonna get trapped behind a school bus and just might commit arson."

"Drive safe."

She snorts. "Please. I'm invincible until at least forty."

I tie off the last place card, and stack it with the others. The ink smudged on my fingers forces my lips to tilt in a small smile. Willa pauses, eyes flicking over the craziness that is today before moving over me.

"You good here?" She asks.

"I've got it." I assure her.

She studies me for half a second longer than necessary. "You know you don't have to keep yourself this busy to avoid thinking."

"I'm not avoiding," I say, too fast. "And this is our busy season, I didn't plan these weddings."

"You absolutely are avoiding," Willa replies, not missing a beat. I shoot her a look, but she just leans in and kisses my cheek. "If he texts, don't overthink it."

"Willa," I groan, rolling my eyes.

"Don't say my name like that," she says, already backing toward the door. "It's been days. Don't turn wanting something into a whole damn project."

She shoulders her delivery bag and slips out the door. The bell chimes softly behind her.

I reach for a spool of ribbon and the bell rings once again.

I don't look up right away—hands still full with twine and the place cards for the McAllister wedding. "Hi, I'll be right with you—"

I glance toward the door.

And immediately wish I hadn't.

Of course. Of fucking course.

Chase and Eva are waltzing in here.

She's in heels no sane person wears before noon and a ridiculous coat that belongs on stage. He's got one hand on her waist, the other already halfway to a wave, smug carved into every inch of his face.

My stomach drops straight through the floor.

Chase grins, all smug charm and fake surprise. "Didn't think you'd still be behind the counter. Figured you'd have someone else handling the messy parts by now."

I don't answer.

Eva's sunglasses stay on. She doesn't even bother with a fake smile. She takes in the shop, the mess on the counter, the flowers, the dusting of chalk and smudged ink on my hands.

"Well," she says, drawing the word out like it's flavored with pity. "Still doing the whole... *crafty little dreamer* thing, huh?"

I stand up a little straighter. Wipe my hands on my apron. "Can I help you with something?"

Chase gives me that easy grin. The one he used to wear

every night when he came home, like he was doing *me* a favor just by showing up. The politician's smile. Polished. Practiced. Hollow as hell.

"Thought we'd do our civic duty," he says, all charm. "Shop local. Be neighborly."

He says it as if he's not the deputy mayor now, as if he doesn't have a staffer for this kind of thing, or a damn intern who could've bought a bouquet and posted it to his campaign socials. But no. He came himself. With Eva on his arm and something to prove.

I stare at him. "Didn't realize playing hometown hero meant interrupting people who actually work for a living."

He laughs too loud. The sound fills the shop, forced and familiar, as if this is friendly banter instead of trespassing.

"You've still got that spark," he says. "Knew you'd do well owning something for your little writing passion. Even said so, remember?"

You also said you loved me. You also married my sister. So no, Chase, I don't put much fucking stock in your compliments anymore.

He's looking around the shop like he's never seen it before, like he's surprised it isn't covered in cobwebs and grief. "Nice setup. Bet it's a hell of a lot easier than real work."

I arch a brow. "This place is a business, not a hobby."

He waves a hand. "You know what I mean. It's cute. You and Willa. Working together."

There it is. *Cute.* The way he used to describe my dreams. The way he talked about my art when we were married. Like it was a phase I'd grow out of once I got serious about being his wife.

I don't flinch. "And you? Still pretending you're the second coming of small-town government?"

He grins wider, proud. "Deputy Mayor's got a nice ring to it."

I nod, slow and give him an inquisitive look, like I'm studying him. "Almost makes people forget what a coward you are."

He flinches enough for me to feel a ping of satisfaction. I'm over his bullshit.

Eva jumps in fast, trying to smooth everything over. "Valentine's rush, right? Figured you'd be buried in petals and panicking quite a bit."

My smile doesn't move. "We're doing fine."

Chase leans in, elbows on the counter like this is some casual catch up. Moments of reality are easily erased in favor of his usual delusion. "I meant what I said, Edie. It's really impressive. What you've built here. I always knew you'd soar through the clouds."

"You didn't know shit," I say, calm as I can manage.

He laughs like we're sharing something. "Come on. Don't be like that. I was proud of you, even at the end."

I don't blink. "There wasn't an end, Chase. You transitioned before it ever really began."

He has the audacity to wince. "It wasn't like that."

"It was exactly like that," I say.

Eva shifts next to him—and I catch it—that little twitch in her jaw. She's not looking at me anymore. She's looking at him.

Chase tries to recover. "Look, things didn't go the way we planned, but that doesn't mean I didn't care about you."

"You didn't care," I say. "You collected. You used. And now you're bored all over again."

His smile falters.

Eva cuts in, voice tighter. "We're not bored. We're married."

His jaw works, but no sound comes out.

I let out a surprised, boisterous laugh. "Oh. I get it now. You wanted to see if I'd fall apart. See if I'd still look at you and melt. Sorry to disappoint."

Chase blinks, not used to me smiling when he's the one trying to control the narrative.

I keep going. "You really thought I'd be upset, didn't you? That I'd see you and fall apart wanting to tell you how much I love you. Maybe cry a little. Say your name like it still means something in my life. Or even that I would be ecstatic to see you."

His smile falters.

I shrug. "Guess you'll have to find your ego somewhere else."

He doesn't answer. That's the thing about men like Chase. They don't know what to do when you're not crawling back. When you're fine. Better, even, without them.

I nod. "I'm not mad. I'm not broken. I'm just not yours anymore. Actually... I don't think I ever was. And that's fine by me. I'm happy now."

Eva shifts, like she's finally seeing what's always been there. She's lesser than me.

Her jaw tightens. Her hand slips from his arm. "We should go," she says, already stepping back. Her voice tilts toward lightness, like this was all just a fun little stop. "You've got that meeting downtown, remember?"

I lean back on my heels, folding the ribbon in my hands. "Wouldn't want you to be late. Politics waits for no man. Or his plus one."

She doesn't answer. Chase's gaze lingers a second too long.

The door swings open again.

Nash steps inside. He really picked the perfect time to join our little party.

Chase tries to clap him on the shoulder on the way out. "Grady. Small town, huh?"

Nash doesn't slow. Just tips his chin and says, "Get smaller every time you open your mouth."

Then he walks past him, into the shop fully, like Chase never existed.

He looks around once, then finds me. His mouth tips into a smile. "Hey."

This is something I love. Simple and easy with no hoops to jump through.

"Hey," I say back, trying not to sound too relieved at having him here right now. The smile that pulls at my lips is all heart.

A throat clears behind him.

Chase.

Still in the doorway. He didn't leave. He steps toward the counter again, Eva a step behind, stiff as ever.

"Oh, don't let us interrupt," Chase says, tone too perky to be real. "Didn't realize you two were... this."

I tilt my head. "This what, Chase?"

He smirks, smug sliding in. "Didn't figure you for someone who goes for grease-stained second place."

Nash doesn't flinch. "Didn't peg you for someone who'd marry his wife's sister. But here we are."

Chase laughs, brittle. Eva freezes beside him.

He tries to smooth it over. "We're all grown ups here. No need to get awkward."

"You're the one circling the counter," I say, not moving.

Nash shifts slightly, but his eyes stay on Chase. He's letting me handle it. He's got my back if I need it. On standby.

His bravado cracks, the words spewing out of his mouth faster than he can control them. "Don't hit on my wife."

Eva gasps.

Nash raises his eyebrows. "I'm not. Your wife is behind you."

Chase's face shutters. Eva's eyes flick to him, full of disbelief.

"Let's go," she says quietly, voice suddenly fragile, broken.

But Chase doesn't move.

"Door's behind you," Nash adds. "In case you forgot again."

Eva tugs his arm. This time, he follows. The bell chimes one last time.

Nash shifts his weight, eyes flicking to the door before coming back to me. "Sorry if I overstepped again."

"You didn't," I say, pulse jumping because it's just us now. "Thank you for letting me handle it."

He nods.

I start toward the cooler. "I don't even know what I ever saw in him," I mutter. "God, I really thought I loved him. I was such an idiot."

My fingers brush the cooler door. I don't open it.

"I don't know what you saw in him, either," he says, coming close and stopping behind me. "But I know what I saw in you when I was twelve."

I freeze. He doesn't wait for me to turn around. "You were wearing those muddy boots and yelling at that boy in

86

the creek for catching frogs in a mason jar. Said they couldn't breathe in there."

I look back at him.

"And I remember thinking," he adds, a smile tugging at the corner of his mouth, "She's got a soft heart and hard elbows. God better help anyone who tries to keep her in a tiny little box."

I can't break away from his eyes. He's about to break me. I can feel it.

"You gave me your ring that day," he adds. "The bread tie one, bent in a loop. I complimented it and you said it couldn't grant all of my wishes unless I said yes to all of my heart's desires. So I said yes. When you forgot about it a week later, I never did." He shrugs one shoulder. "Still have it. Top drawer of my dresser, tucked in an old Altoids tin."

I blink hard.

He lifts the other shoulder. "You wanna know what I saw in you, Eden? I saw forever. Even when we were just kids."

I don't think. Don't panic or second guess. I just move.

Three steps until I am right in front of him.

And I kiss him.

Like it's always been him.

If I'm being honest, it always was.

CHAPTER NINE

Eden

B y eight a.m., we're already behind. So behind it feels like we will never be able to catch up.

It's the day before Valentine's Day, and wouldn't you know it's on a Saturday. Like the universe looked at our to-do list and gave us the middle finger.

There's glitter in my bra, eucalyptus oil on my wrists, and I've rewritten one place card three times because I can't remember how to spell *Isabelle* for the life of me.

Willa is hauling a box of sweetheart roses from the cooler to her work bench.

"I hate these arrangements," she mutters.

"No you don't," I call back.

"I hate them this time of year," she quips at me.

I can't lie, I hate them too.

We hired three drivers for today, thank God. Otherwise I think Willa might've just launched herself into traffic.

"This is abuse," she grits, ducking under a garland to reach the cooler. "We should unionize against ourselves."

"We are the union," I mutter. "And also the problem."

The shop is a war zone of love. Tissue paper and ribbon

tails on every flat surface. Candles, corsages, three different order sheets taped to the register. We've got two weddings tomorrow. Twenty seven Valentine's deliveries. Also, zero sanity left between us.

Willa reappears, dropping a bouquet onto my workstation with a thud. "This one's yours."

I blink. "I don't remember a last minute order that I have to do."

"You didn't take this one. Someone sent it." She taps the tag with a smug finger. "To Eden Taylor."

I freeze.

Slowly, I unwrap the butcher paper.

Cosmos. White anemones. Lavender. Just a little off center, just a little wild. No red. No forced romance. Whoever this is from was super thoughtful to what I would love.

I don't have to read the card to know who would be thoughtful enough for this.

I open the card.

For the girl who always made my heart bloom.

—N

"Oh my God," Willa whispers, coming into my space like a firecracker. "You're gonna marry him."

"Willa," I say, voice catching as I think about what he is saying to me.

"Cosmos? White anemones? Lavender?" Willa holds the bouquet like it's the crown jewels. "This man built a whole thesis on your heart in stems and flower theory. And he *handwrote* the note? Eden. Babe. If you don't marry him, someone will. I hope that someone will be you."

I can't speak. I can barely look away from the bouquet. I press my fingers to the note and read it again.

"He remembered I hate red roses," I whisper.

"Are you really that surprised?"

"I guess I'm so used to no one knowing," I say.

"No," Willa responds. "You're used to Chase not caring. But this is Nash we're talking about. He kept that fucking ring you made him when we were twelve. He remembers everything about you."

She's right. I am thinking of Chase. He never took the time to remember or care. Always gave me red roses on every holiday. Valentine's Day, birthdays, whatever he needed them for. Even apologies were red roses. I always fucking hated them.

Willa doesn't say anything. She's always been team Nash. But when I told her about the ring, she practically melted.

I shake my head, but I'm smiling.

"Yeah," I mutter, a little breathless. "I think I'm gonna marry him."

Willa pauses, bouquet halfway wrapped. Her lips break into the slowest, smuggest grin I've ever seen. "Well it's about damn time."

I roll my eyes, but I'm smiling. Can't help it.

"You tell him yet?"

"Not in words."

Willa snorts. "Girl, you *kissed* him. He probably went home and started Googling venues."

Before I can respond, there is a huge bang. The front door slams open, crashing against the wall so hard the glass shudders in the frame.

Both of us jump.

Storm clouds are officially in the shop. One of which is in designer heels.

Eva's back. Without Chase this time.

Willa doesn't move. "Well. Shit."

"Okay. Come on in," I say, sarcastically as she storms toward us.

"I knew it," she says, breathless. "I *knew* you'd do this."

Neither of us speaks.

Her eyes dart between me and the bouquet on the counter.

I see it. I see the moment she assumes the bouquet is from someone that it isn't.

"Oh my God," she laughs, as she falls back a step, unsteady on her feet. "You really don't know when to quit, do you?"

Still nothing. I give her no room to assume or hurt me. Eva has this way where she feels like she can attack me if she sees a weakness. Usually, I would be anxious about everything I do.

Now, I just don't care. I'm over her crazy bullshit.

She takes a step closer, pointing to the flowers like they're some kind of evidence. "You think I don't see it? The timing? The little looks? A bouquet, Eden? Really? That's your move now? You're trying to hook him into coming back to you."

Willa is about to speak, but I give her a little shake of my head. I want to see where this is going.

Eva's voice rises. "Let me guess. He just happened to stop by. Slipped you a note. A little *valentine*, right? Right when things are finally good for me."

Her gaze is laser focused on me now, chest heaving.

"You've always done this," she spits. "Play the quiet little mouse. Let everyone underestimate you while you take what you want."

She shakes her head, pacing. "And on top of that, you don't even want him. That's the part that kills me. You just can't stand that he picked me. That I *won*."

Something inside me settles. A cold chill runs down my spine. Chase said he wanted to win. Beat Nash. Eva wanted to beat me. Everything about this shit is a game. Love should never be one. You should never play with someone's heart.

"He still talks about you," she blurts, like it's a secret she's kept in too long. "He acts like he doesn't mean anything by it. I know it though. I see the way he looks at his phone scrolling through pictures. You're still in there. In his head."

She laughs again. Okay this bitch is crazier than I thought.

"But that doesn't mean anything," she rushes on. "Men do that. It's nostalgia. Habit. He married *me*. He built a life with *me*."

Her eyes flick to the bouquet again—soft petals, handwritten card, everything Nash.

But she sees Chase.

"This?" She scoffs. "This is nothing. Guilt flowers. A phase. He'll wake up. He always does."

Willa finally speaks. She's had enough of this lunatic rambling. She tilts her head, smirking like she's watching a reality show spiral into a finale night meltdown.

"Wooow," she says, slow and dry. "You really thought these were from *Chase*?"

Eva blinks, caught mid rant.

Willa gestures to the bouquet—soft and stunning and unmistakably Eden. "Those are cosmos. And white anemones. And lavender. Do you really think *Chase* knows or even cares about the difference between a peony and a parking ticket?"

Eva's eyes widen before she narrows them toward Willa.

"They're from Nash," Willa adds. "Who, in case you

forgot, doesn't need pity flowers or borrowed husbands to feel like a man."

"Take a breath, Eva," I say, trying my best to hold in the laugh bubbling up my throat. "Chase is all yours. Every slimy, spineless inch of him."

Eva laughs. She is trying to save face at this point.

"Okay," she says, nodding too fast. "Okay, sure. Nash. Fine. That makes sense."

Yeah, she doesn't believe any of it.

She gestures vaguely between me and the bouquet. "So what, now he's your big hero? The one who sends flowers and plays house? That's... that's sweet. Really. Temporary, but sweet."

Willa doesn't respond. I don't either.

Eva keeps going. She always does. "Because this—" she waves a hand at the shop, the flowers, me, "—this isn't real life. It's nostalgia. It's unfinished business. People get confused by that."

She swallows, and smooths down her coat. It's an old habit she's had since we were kids. Whenever she'd be getting in trouble for something, she'd always try to fix her appearance instead of facing whatever the punishment may have been.

"Chase and I?" She says, softer now, more composed. "We're solid. We've made something unique. You wouldn't understand that part."

I finally look at her. "Eva," I say calmly, "I understand it better than you think."

Her smile twitches. "You just think you do. You always did. You always thought you were better, kinder even. More... deserving of all this."

She laughs again, but it's brittle. "But men don't want

that forever. They want excitement. They want someone who pushes back."

Willa exhales through her nose, but still says nothing.

Eva nods to herself. "He'll come back around. He always does. He just needs to remember who chose him first."

I set the ribbon down at last. Meet her eyes. "No," I say gently. "He needs to remember who he *is*. And that's not my problem anymore."

Eva stares at me. Her face twists. "You always act so above it all. Like you're better than the rest of us."

I glance at Willa, who raises an eyebrow like *is she serious?*

"Keep telling yourself that," Eva spits. "Keep pretending this is some moral victory and not just you being pathetic."

She doesn't wait for a response this time. She spins on her heel and the door nearly slams behind her.

The bell's still echoing when I grab my phone.

"I need to see him," I say.

Willa doesn't even ask who. She wipes her hands on a dish towel and nods. "I'll call Wes."

He picks up on the second ring, mouth full—probably mid lunch. "What'd she do now?"

"Is Nash at the shop?" Willa asks, already digging for her keys.

"No. He took the day. Said something about needing to work on his house and wanting some solitude."

I step in. "Wes. I need his address."

There's a pause. I know this is his version of hesitation.

"Please," I say. "I'm not gonna break his heart."

With a dramatic sigh and some muttered cursing, he

rattles it off. Willa writes it on the back of a receipt and hands it to me with a raised brow.

"Go," she says. "And don't you dare half ass this."

I'm already moving. The bouquet still sits on the counter. There is so much I need to tell him. Starting with I've loved him since I gave him that bread tie ring and never stopped.

The drive feels longer than it is.

My pulse doesn't slow down the whole way there—hands tight on the wheel, mouth dry, brain racing.

Unless Wes or Willa called him, he doesn't know I'm coming. He doesn't know I'm showing up with every beat of my heart ready to say yes to him seven plus years too late.

By the time I turn down the drive, my breath's gone and I'm half ready to throw up. In the best way.

His old truck's parked outside. And the lights are on inside. It feels like a home, or at least it's well on it's way to being one.

I don't knock like a normal person. I run up the steps, heart in my throat, and bang on the door with the flat of my hand. I know I look insane, like something awful is chasing me. Like I'm the main character—or the girl about to die—in the horror movie.

It opens almost immediately.

He is wearing a hoodie with paint on the sleeve and socks that don't match. He looks lived in. Happy and completely comfortable. His black hair is messy. He is not trying to impress whoever could possibly come over. He just is who he is.

And I blurt it before I can stop myself. "I love you."

His mouth parts, like maybe he wasn't expecting it like that. But I don't stop. I can't.

"I love you," I say again, out of breath and halfway laughing. "I should've said it the second I saw you again. I should've said it years ago. And if you don't feel the same, that's fine, really—except it's not. Because I've loved you since I was twelve years old, Nash. Since the day I gave you that bread tie ring and made you promise to never lose it. You didn't. You kept it."

My voice wavers, but I don't stop.

"I've loved you through everything. Through that dumb phase where I pretended I didn't care, when all I wanted was for you to notice. Through every awful moment with Chase. Through the wedding I shouldn't have gone through with. Through the years we didn't speak. I loved you when I hated myself for it, and I love you now."

I take a breath that shakes all the way down. My heart's in my throat. My hands are cold.

"I love you," I whisper. "And I don't want to pretend I don't anymore."

A voice cuts in behind him.

"Who's at the door?"

Everything in me stops. Not stutters. Not skips.

Stops cold.

I blink once my stomach is already sinking, heavy and hollow in my feet.

Behind him, I catch the edge of movement. Blonde hair. Bare feet. A mug in her hand.

My lungs forget how to work.

Of course. Of *course*. I drive across town, pour my heart out on his front step like it's some damn fairytale, and he's got company.

Female company.

God, Eden. You really thought that you even had a chance.

"Oh," I breathe, stepping back, hands suddenly ice. "I'm—sorry. I didn't realize—" I laugh once, trying to stay calm. "I thought—"

I start to turn.

But he reaches for my hand.

"Eden," he says. "I love you too. I always have."

I point dumbly at the house. "But—"

He shakes his head, already stepping toward me. "That's Tasha. Wes and I basically adopted her as our little sister while we were in California. She's staying with me for a few days, helping with the move. Moving here herself, actually."

I blink. "Little sister."

He gives a small, almost breathless laugh. "Yeah. So if you're done planning how this whole thing ends, I'd really like to get back to the part where you said you love me."

I open my mouth. Nothing comes out.

Nash reaches for my hands, wraps them in his. They are warm and sure. "You thought that I wouldn't love you back?" I can hear the awe in his voice. "Eden, I have loved you since you stormed into that creek in muddy boots and made me swear we'd never keep frogs in jars like that other kid did."

My heart flips. He pulls me closer.

"And I've said yes, every damn day since. Even when you weren't mine. Even when I thought you never would be."

His forehead touches mine.

"You're it for me. You always have been. I've waited

seven years to say it again, and I'll wait as long as it takes... but I swear to you, Eden, I'm not going anywhere."

That's it. That's the moment. The part where the air shifts. Where my chest breaks wide open. Where everything I've been holding back rushes forward.

I kiss him, and every part of me is finally breathing again.

My heart has been waiting for this—for him—for years.

I loved him then.

I love him now.

And I'll love him in every version of this life we get.

CHAPTER TEN

Nash

E den's still in my arms, breathing hard. So am I.
We're finally here. Together.

A throat clears behind me. She flinches. I turn around.

"Don't mind me," Tasha says from the doorway. "Just over here trying not to vomit from all the sexual tension."

Eden jerks like she's been electrocuted. Tasha turns around and walks to the counter with her bag slung over her shoulder, smirking like she's the one who just made a house call to Cupid. She grabs her keys before coming back to us.

"You two love birds enjoy yourselves," she says, heading for her car. "Don't break anything. Or each other."

Eden hides her face in my shirt. I can sense a full body flush happening. I can feel her trying not to laugh.

Tasha stops at the door, gives me a look. "You're welcome, by the way."

"For what?"

She gives me a playful shove with a grin. "For leaving so you get to spend some time with your girl."

She leaves without waiting for a reply.

Eden lifts her head, still smiling. "Did she seriously just say that?"

I nod once. "She did."

"She always like this?"

I tilt my head. "That was her being gentle."

Eden laughs, soft and surprised.

"There's a story there," she says. "With her."

I nod once. "Yeah."

She stands there, not saying a word, but I can feel the question she's not asking.

"Tasha showed up at one of our shows," I say. "Met her on a job trip with Wes. She was working out of this back alley garage in California. Didn't have any family that mattered. She was all alone."

Eden watches me like she already knows where this is going.

"She was mouthy, smarter than the guy who ran the place, and fixing bikes like she was born with a wrench in her hand. Said she'd been bouncing around since she aged out of the system."

Eden's hands rest lightly at my waist. She doesn't interrupt.

"I offered her a job. She showed up three days later with a duffel, a clipboard, and a list of everything wrong with our shop. Never left." Eden doesn't say anything. "She's not blood," I say. "But she's ours."

She steps in closer, and her body presses against mine like gravity decided something for both of us. "I like how you talk about her," she says. "Like you don't realize you're proud."

I glance down at her mouth. "I don't say things I don't mean."

"I know."

She lifts her face. Her lips are inches from mine. "You gonna kiss me again?"

"No."

Her brows flick, caught between amusement and confusion.

"Not unless you ask," I murmur.

She slides her fingers up under my shirt, over bare skin. Looks me dead in the eye.

"Nash," she whispers. "Kiss me."

We walk to the kitchen, lips tangled with each other.

I kiss her like I'm starved. Like she's the first glass of a cold drink on a hot, humid, Mississippi summer day.

There's no hesitation in her. No second guessing in me. Her mouth meets mine like it remembers me, like it never forgot, and I sink into it with the kind of pressure that says this isn't a question anymore.

Not awkward like our first kiss. This one feels special. I need to feel every damn second of it. Need to memorize the way she tastes. I never want this to end.

She sighs into my mouth and grips my shirt like she needs something to hold on to, and I do the only thing I know how to do right now. I kiss her deeper.

My hand slides into her hair, tilts her face to mine, and I take her bottom lip between my teeth, not hard. Just enough to make sure she knows that this isn't a mistake. This isn't a maybe.

It's always been her.

"Nash," she breathes, and I smile against her mouth. My name on her lips, in that breathy voice, it's almost enough to undo me right here.

I don't let her pull away. I loop an arm around her waist and sling her up, hips landing hard on the cold granite. Her legs dangle. I press into her thighs, feeling her electric jerk.

She threads her fingers in my hair, hauling me closer, and I let out a low promise of a growl.

"Goddamn," I murmur, my mouth at her jaw, breath dragging as I press closer. "Been thinking about this for years."

I kiss down her neck, slow and hungry, my teeth grazing the skin right where her pulse kicks up under me. She gasps, and I lean in harder. I pick her up and put her on the counter.

With one tug I lift her shirt over her head. The air hits her and goosebumps ripple across her bare skin. I stare, memorizing every curve. My callused thumbs trace her ribcage, then slide up to palm her breast. When I squeeze, she whines.

"You're going to bruise," I warn, fingernail tracing the area she hit the counter.

She arches into my touch, breath catching when I roll her nipple between my fingers. I lower my mouth, brushing that same spot, soft for a second.

I bite—not rough, just enough to draw a sound from her throat.

Her fingers tighten in my hair, and she pulls me closer instead of pushing me off.

That sound she makes is surrender.

I unbutton her jeans with one hand. She claws at my belt but I catch her wrists, pressing them into the cabinet so hard she can't budge.

She gasps, eyes wide. "Control freak much?"

I lean in, lips brushing her ear. "Absolutely."

She lets out a breath, half a laugh.

"You seem to like it," I murmur, voice low and rough.

I lean in for another kiss. I know she is starting to seethe a bit. My tongue parts her lips and tastes her. I want to memorize every shiver so I can replay it forever. I shift, using my forearm to keep her arms trapped, free hand yanking her jeans until they bunch at her knees. She hooks her ankles around me, grinding, and I shudder against her.

"Careful," I growl against her ear, dragging my teeth along her throat. "You're making it hard to be gentle."

Her breath shudders out.

"Who said I want gentle?"

That does it.

My own jeans go down in a yank and my cock springs free, slick with precome. I spit in my palm and stroke once, twice, never breaking eye contact. I position myself. "Tell me you want it."

"Fuck me," she hisses back. "Now."

I plunge in with one savage thrust, bottoming out. She screams, head snapping back. I don't pause. I piston in, each push punishing, the wet symphony of her arousal filling the room. She arches, and clamps her teeth into my shoulder. That is going to leave a mark.

Her wrists fly free and she rips at my shirt. I roam her body—kneading breasts, hauling ass, fingers prying her thighs wide. She claws my back, and I roar against her neck.

"Look at me while I fuck you," I command.

I murmur her name and she looks up at me, eyes wild, like I'm the only thing that matters in her world.

I slow down, rolling my hips until I feel the spot that makes her jolt beneath me. She arches, breath catching like I've hit something deep and perfect, so I do it again— harder this time. Her legs tighten around me, her body clenching like she's close, and I swear I feel her pulse against my cock, begging for more.

Her pussy clamps down and I groan, grip her chin, and kiss her through her climax as she spasms around me. She's mine. I follow right after, cursing low as I spill inside, my hips trembling on hers.

She's still shaking when I pull out, her skin hot, breath coming fast, chest pressed tight against mine.

I don't let her go.

I kiss her shoulder. Her hands are still in my hair like she can't—or won't—stop touching me. I lift her. She wraps around me easy, like it's natural. We fit together perfectly.

"I'll give you the tour later," I murmur against her neck as I carry her down the hall.

She laughs against my throat and I swear it shoots straight through me. I want her again, already. But more than that... I want her *here*.

I carry her into the bedroom and drop her on the mattress. She bounces once, hair a mess across my pillow, eyes on me.

And fuck, she's beautiful.

Not something far away I had to pretend I didn't want. She's right here—flushed, loose limbed, still catching her breath—and I get to see every inch of her.

"Well," she says, wry with a smirk curving at the edges of her mouth. "We can start with the bed."

My cock twitches.

I shake my head.

"Smart mouth's gonna get you in trouble," I say, my voice husky as I crawl over her, hands already sliding beneath her thighs.

"Maybe I'm counting on it," she says, mouth curved, eyes full of want.

This time, I take her slow. We have all the time in the world to explore each other.

CHAPTER ELEVEN

Eden

The smell of coffee gets me out of bed.

I don't remember falling asleep, but I remember everything else—his mouth, his hands, the way he said my name. Over and over again. My body hums with soreness in all the right places.

I tug one of his shirts over my head. It hangs past my thighs and smells like cedar and engine oil. I love it.

The house is still dim when I pad into the kitchen. Nash stands at the counter, back to me, already dressed—black tee, dark jeans, boots on. He's packing something into a small cooler. Sandwiches, maybe. There's a thermos beside him. A folded paper towel. He moves like this is normal. Like we've done this a hundred times.

He turns slightly, just enough to glance at me. His mouth curves, barely. *Good morning* without saying it.

I move toward the coffee like gravity's pulling me.

"Didn't mean to sleep in," I murmur, still hoarse.

"You didn't," he says. "Didn't want to wake you."

The clock on the stove flashes the time.

Shit.

I freeze mid pour.

"I'm late," I say, already turning. "I was supposed to open. Willa's going to kill me."

I don't see his reaction—I'm already sprinting back down the hall, heart racing, hair a mess, his shirt still half on my body.

I yank on yesterday's jeans and pull my sweater over my head without bothering with a mirror. My bra is somewhere. I don't care, I'll get it later. I grab my phone, shove it in my pocket, and nearly trip on my boots on the way back to the kitchen.

He's still there, calm as ever, standing in the kitchen while I ricochet off the walls like a cartoon character running off a cliff.

"I texted Willa," he says as I reach for my bag. "Told her you'd be late. She said the shop's covered."

I freeze with my hand on the strap.

I try not to panic at the thought of him texting Willa. Nash is different. He is not taking control like Chase did.

I turn to face him. "This..." I say, my voice catching on my own spit. "I want to keep this private. For now. Until we figure it out."

Nash straightens, just slightly. His eyes meet mine. The look on his face breaks my heart."I'm not hiding you," I add quickly. "I'm not ashamed. I just—"

"Okay," he says while trying to hide the frown on his face. "Private's fine."

I look at his lips. I know that he's not happy about this.

He sets his thermos in the cooler and zips it shut. "Willa already knows."

I let out a breath. "Yeah. Willa doesn't count."

He raises a brow.

"I mean... I want it private from the town. From Chase. From Eva."

His jaw shifts. "You think they'll ruin it?"

I nod, throat tight. "I'm happy, really happy. I don't want them near that."

That finally makes him smile. Not wide. Just enough. "You're allowed to want something good," he says.

"Yeah..." I trail off. "But I don't want someone bad in the mix."

The bell over the door chimes as I step into Ink & Stem, hoping I can sneak in, make it to the back, and pretend I've been here since sunrise.

No such luck.

Willa's already behind the counter, arms crossed, one brow arched so high it's practically above her hairline.

"Someone didn't come home last night," she says sweetly. Ugh she is weaponizing her sing song voice. She definitely wants to know everything.

I drop my bag by the worktable and try to keep my face neutral. "Hi."

"Hope you got some," she adds. "And I *really* hope it was fun. Because I opened the shop alone and had to console Mrs. Talbot when she cried over a misspelled 'forever.'"

Apparently, Mrs. Talbot showed up again this morning in full bridal mother meltdown mode. She's been in here every day since placing the order like they're the only things we have going on.

Four hundred invitations. Programs. Menus. All hand designed. It'll take a month, minimum.

Thank God we finally got the new calligraphy printer. But even then, she insists on one perfect Eden original before anything gets approved. I only do one at a time. My hands are cramping more every day.

Willa says she cried over a misspelled *forever*. It wasn't misspelled. It was correct. She's the one that chose the style..

I wince. "I owe you a coffee."

"Oh, you owe me more than that. You owe me *details.* Because your mouth says good morning but your hair says 'I got thoroughly fucked by Motorcycle Brooding Hotness.'"

I choke on air. "Willa."

"Don't *Willa* me. I've seen post orgasm Eden before and baby, you're glowing. Well the post orgasm Eden I've seen is nothing like that. You've got Nash Grady all over you."

"Please stop," I mutter, dragging a hand down my face as Willa dissolves into another dramatic retelling.

She rounds the counter, zero hesitation. "Don't get weird and guilty now. You're allowed to enjoy it. Unless it was terrible, in which case I will go down to that garage and threaten him with a peony bouquet."

"It wasn't terrible," I say, too casually and Willa narrows her eyes. I knew this wouldn't be enough for her.

Her grin slips into something gentler. "Good. Because you deserve not terrible."

I lean against the counter, fingers brushing a stack of pressed paper. "It wasn't just sex."

That stops her. Her eyes widen just a little, and her voice dips. "No?"

I shake my head. "He told me he loved me. Well more like said it back. After I told him."

"Oh, *shit*," she whispers.

"Yeah."

Willa throws herself into the nearest chair, hand to her chest like she's overwhelmed. "So we're talking confessions and naked vulnerability now? What's next, shared Spotify playlists? Coordinated groceries?"

I groan. "You're impossible."

"*You're* in love. Which, to be fair, I already knew. But it's nice to see you finally catching up."

I blow out a breath. "I just... I don't know how to do this part."

"What part?"

"The part where it's real. It all feels perfect. But it can't be. Nothing ever is."

She gets up and walks straight to me, nudging me with her elbow, voice against my ear. "Eden. You already survived the worst part of love. What's left is rebuilding. And Nash? That man looks at you like he'd walk through a bed of nails barefoot just to hear you laugh."

I press my lips together, heart rattling in my chest. "I told him I want to keep it private for now. From the town. From Chase. Eva."

Willa nods. There is no judgment in her eyes. "Smart."

"I don't want them near it. I'm happy, Willa. I want five seconds to be happy without someone trying to destroy it."

"Then take your five seconds. Hell, take fifty. Protect it. But don't shut down just because it's good. Good doesn't mean fragile."

I glance down, noticing grease smudged on my wrist. It's probably from Nash's hands on me last night. I don't scrub it off. Instead, I run my finger over it. "I think I'm already in deep."

Willa beams. "Good. Maybe now you'll admit that the way he looks at you makes your knees go all gooey."

"It does not."

"Bitch, yes it does."

A laugh slips out before I can stop it. "You're a menace."

"I'm your menace. Now tell me everything. How was it?"

"I am not giving you a play by play."

"You don't have to. Just... what did he say? Right before he took your pants off?"

I flush instantly. "Willa."

"Come *on*. For me?"

I glance at her, cheeks turning a bright shade of red.

She freezes, hand to her chest. "Come on! Give me something. That man was forged in a steel mill and sent back in time to ruin you."

"Stop." I say giving her the universal lips are sealed sign.

"*RUIN*. YOU."

We're both laughing now, clearing the fog away from thinking about Chase or Eva.

The bell over the door rings.

Willa freezes, eyes flicking past me.

"Gross," she mutters, there's an edge to it that tells me I'm about to become very unhappy.

I don't need to turn. My whole body tightens.

"Ladies," Chase says smoothly, stepping inside, all swagger and entitlement. "Hope I'm not interrupting."

Willa shifts, folding her arms across her chest. "We're closed."

He laughs like she's joking. "Thought I'd stop by. My

wife's charity event's coming up, and we're doing custom menus."

I finally look up. His smile is blinding. There's a man underneath it, but I stopped knowing who that was years ago.

They didn't order it from me. Unless he's trying to now. Please for the love of fuck don't try to order it now.

"We're booked solid through the week," I say, trying to keep my tone even. "Try someone else."

He tsks, all mock disappointment. "Come on, Edie. Thought you'd be happy to help."

He does want to order it from me. Nope. Not happening.

"I'm sure Eva can find another calligrapher that would be much more willing to take your... business," I say.

Willa snorts under her breath.

He walks closer, gaze flicking between us. "Funny timing, though. Been hearing some things lately. About who you've been spending time with."

"Do you mean Nash?" I surprise him, Willa, and myself with how easy that was to say. Especially since I just said I wanted to keep our relationship to ourselves.

Willa raises a brow. "Say it, Chase. Say the name of the man you used to call your brother before he got too good to be around you anymore."

Chase shifts, that fake casual smile barely holding. "Look, I get it. It's Nash. I mean... he was my best friend. I know how he is. He's... intense. I'm just saying that it feels a little sudden, that's all."

"Sudden," I echo, tilting my head. "You mean like how you proposed to my sister before the ink on the divorce was even dry? Pot, meet kettle."

Willa slaps the counter. "Oh we are *spicy* today. Is this what post Nash glow looks like? I love it here."

Chase holds up his hands. "I'm not trying to fight. I'm just saying I know you. And this thing with Nash. It's just not you. You're not a... bad boy girl."

"I'm not a compulsive liar girl," I say sweetly. "Yet, here you stand."

Willa beams. "That's what we call growth, baby."

"I'm just looking out for you," Chase adds, a little desperate now. "You don't need to do this just to prove something. You deserve better than that."

"I told Eva I don't want you back." I sit on a stool and cross my arms. "When she came here to confront me. I'm going to tell you the same thing. I don't want you. Scram, little man."

His whole body stills.

"She didn't tell you?" I ask, tilting my head. That is interesting. "Wow. Guess she's too busy curating her perfect life to mention that little visit."

Willa whistles through her teeth. "Man. She left that off the vision board?"

Chase fumbles. "That's not what this is about."

"Oh no," Willa says. "Please continue. I'm dying to hear your thoughts on Eden's love life. Again."

"You think Nash is some kind of savior?" He snaps. "You think he's gonna stay?"

"I think he's not you," I say. "That and as *deputy* mayor, thought you would have known that he bought a house."

Willa bows like it's theater. "And the mic has been dropped."

Chase stares at me like he's searching for something he left behind.

"You're making a mistake," he mutters.

I smile. "I already made one. But luckily, he married someone else. Not my problem anymore."

Chase flinches before he storms out. Stiff and full of hatred.

Willa turns to me, eyes bright. "God. That was better than coffee."

My hands are shaking now that he's gone.

"Still want to keep your love quiet?" She asks gently.

I nod. "I'm not going to hide it, but I'm not going to go out of my way to throw it in their faces. They don't get to be a part of any of my life decisions anymore."

She grins. "Good. Because watching them spiral at the charity event is going to be delicious."

CHAPTER TWELVE

Eden

I hold the blush-pink invitation between two fingers, careful not to smudge the gold foil. Eva's name is splashed across the top in loopy script, and underneath, in sparkly italics, *An Evening to Remember*.

I didn't do the lettering. Pretty sure no one did. It looks expensive and premade... like they paid extra to make it look custom, and still got it wrong.

Willa lounges on the couch, one leg slung over the armrest, chewing on a Twizzler like it's a cigar. "You're going," she says.

"I never said I wasn't."

"You've been sighing at that thing for ten minutes."

I flip it over. Back again. "It's a charity event. Not a duel."

"Could be both," she mutters. "But if you're going, go with the man. Bet you five bucks he didn't get an invite. Chasey Boy probably threw a tantrum at the printer just thinking about Nash's name on an one. Probably cried into Eva's mood board and demanded he get a say in that to compensate for his bruised ego."

"I can't just—"

"Call him," she repeats, leveling me with that florist stare that's seen too many breakdowns and wedding disasters to be ignored. "Tell him you're an idiot. Because you are. You're trying to keep something good quiet in a town that never shuts up about the bad. You are letting Chase and Eva live rent free in your head and pretending that they'll be able to ruin it. So yeah—tell him you were wrong. Tell him you want to go with him. And tell him to wear something hot so everyone in town can choke on it."

I don't know if I want to. I have to. Ugh but I don't want to admit that I'm wrong.

I roll my eyes, trying to hide the fact that I'm nervous, but grab my phone anyway.

Because she's right. I was an idiot. It's time I stop acting like what we have is something to hide. We're not children anymore.

My thumb hovers over his name. I take a deep breath and hit it. I can hear a singular ring before he picks up.

"Eden," Nash says, dragging it out just enough to let the grin at the corners of his mouth come through. It feels like he's been waiting all day to say it again.

I swallow. "Hey."

I can almost hear him thinking on the other end. "Everything okay?"

"Yeah," I say, though my heart's beating so loud I'm sure he can hear it through the phone. "Better than okay, actually. I just—I wanted to tell you something. Or ask you something. Or both."

He waits. I hear him chuckle. I'm sure he already knows what's coming.

"I was wrong," I say. "About hiding us. I thought I was protecting something, but I was really just letting other people's opinions decide what I was allowed to be happy about. And I don't want to do that anymore."

His breath hitches, barely audible. "Okay."

"There's this charity thing," I go on. "Tomorrow night. It's Eva's event. Willa and I are going, and I want you to come too. As my date."

"I heard about that." He pauses for just a moment. "You sure you want me there? With you?"

"Yeah." I blow out a breath. "I want to walk in there like I'm proud of what we're rebuilding. Of *you*. Let them whisper. Let Eva grind her teeth. I want it all."

"You wanna scream it from the rooftops, huh?" He asks, then clears his throat, like the words came out faster than he meant them to.

"Don't tempt me," I murmur.

"Too late." I can hear the smile in his voice, and it makes everything feel lighter.

"I'll be there," he says. "And I'll wear something hot."

I laugh, the sound catching in my throat. "Wait—how did you know Willa said that?"

He chuckles. "I know Willa."

"She also said she wants the town to choke on it."

"Sounds about right. Tell her to bring Wes."

Before I can respond, the line clicks. He's already hung up. I lower the phone, smiling like an idiot.

"He says bring Wes," I tell her.

Willa doesn't miss a beat. She snatches her phone off the couch, thumbs flying. "On it."

I raise an eyebrow, but I don't say it out loud. Still, she smirks as she types, all quick fingers and practiced ease that almost passes for casual.

There *was* something with Wes. Everyone knew it.

They were solid, the kind of love that felt lived in and

sure that they are going someplace far. That is until his ex showed up. She wanted him back.

Willa didn't fall apart. Didn't fight for a place in a relationship that suddenly felt like it wasn't hers. She stepped back so that Wes could make the decision himself. But honestly, she was protecting herself.

Wes begged her not to. Said she was being righteous over a choice that wasn't hers to make. But Willa never budged. She said real love meant knowing when to let someone go.

Wes never got over her.

He did go back to his ex. Everyone expected him to, so that's what he did. To everyone, she was the one who got away. But if anyone looked close enough, they'd see that his heart wasn't in it. I wasn't the only one who noticed how long he'd look at Willa, how he'd go out of his way to walk by the shop.

He and his ex only lasted three months before they broke up again.

Willa still loves him. I see it, even when she pretends it doesn't matter.

I don't think he ever stopped loving her either.

"Wills," I say quietly.

She looks up, eyes searching. "I love you."

Her mouth quirks in a wry way that screams Willa. "Not as much as I love you."

The mansion looks exactly how you'd expect when Eva gets to design the party and Chase gets to write the checks.

Oversized floral arrangements that don't match the season. Too many servers. Not enough parking.

Willa and I wait near the valet line, shivering in cocktail dresses and regretting everything.

"Remind me why we're early?" She mutters, adjusting her wrap.

"Because I wanted to make an entrance."

"You wanted to spy on the appetizers."

"Also that."

She bumps her shoulder into mine just as headlights swing toward us. My pulse stumbles.

"They're here," I whisper, and try not to look like I'm about to throw up.

Willa grins, wide and wicked. "Game on."

Nash climbs out of his truck, all broad shoulders, rolled sleeves, and that maddening, slow confidence that makes women stupid. His tie's crooked. I'd bet money that is on purpose. And his hair's a mess in a way that says he didn't try.

He looks good. Sinfully, devastatingly good. My stomach flips. My knees wobble.

"Hey," he says, voice low enough so I know it's just for me.

"Hi." Trying to stay chill is not my forte.

Wes gives Willa a crooked smile. "You clean up all right."

"Don't get excited," she deadpans. "Not gonna happen again until the next reunion."

"Knowing our shithole school," Wes drawls. "That'll probably be in the next two years. If we're lucky that is."

Nash chuckles and slides his hand into mine without asking. It fits so perfectly that I try not to shiver. "Let's head in before someone realizes we're too hot for this party."

I roll my eyes but follow his lead.

We don't even make it to the foyer before a woman with a headset and clipboard materializes like she's guarding a red carpet.

"Names?" She asks, barely looking at us.

"Willa Adair and Eden Taylor," Willa says, already pulling the invite from her clutch. I follow, mirroring her.

Clipboard Woman scans the list, nods, then her gaze flicks behind us to Nash and Wes. "They're not on the list."

"They're with us," Willa says without missing a beat.

"They're not listed as individual guests."

"They're *plus ones*," I cut in, heat rising to my cheeks. I'm over this shit. "These invitations say plus one."

Clipboard Woman hesitates. Clearly, this wasn't covered in her little training session with Eva. She eyes Nash like he might be here to crash the bar and ruin the carpet with his boots.

Willa crosses her arms. "You really gonna turn away the two hottest men at this party? Because Eva forgot how plus ones work?"

Nash leans down, stage whispering to me. "Do I get extra hot points for not punching anyone yet?"

I snort. "So far."

Clipboard Woman sighs and steps aside. "Fine."

Willa shoots her a look so harsh it could slice twill. "Thank you *so* much."

We step inside, heels clicking on marble. Nash takes my hand. I squeeze it once.

Here we go.

We don't even make it ten steps before I feel that prickle across my skin that says I'm being watched, judged, and hated all at the same time.

I look up—Chase. I knew I would see him, I was just hoping I'd have at least a minute before that moment.

He's planted by the champagne tower like he built it himself, smile pulled too tight, fingers clenched around a glass he's not drinking from. The woman next to him is talking—laughing, maybe—but he's not listening. He's locked in.

On me. On Nash's hand around mine.

He doesn't blink. Doesn't flinch. But I see it—right there beneath the smug, beneath the suit. Hatred.

Not just toward Nash. But toward me just as much, maybe even more if I'm honest.

Because I stopped playing the part. Because I walked in with the man he was always afraid I'd choose. Because I look happy.

Eva tries her best to ignore us all.

She's across the room, clinking glasses and tossing rehearsed smiles like confetti. Pretending this is just another flawless evening under her name, that the tension slicing through the room isn't hers to notice. She doesn't look at me. Doesn't look at Nash.

"I'm gonna find the restroom," I say, not quite meeting Willa's eyes.

She studies me for half a second. "You need backup?"

"I'll be quick."

I weave through the crowd, head down, heels biting into the floor with every step toward the hallway near the coat check. Cool air brushes my skin, and for a second, it almost feels like escape.

I just need a minute. One breath without the music, the champagne, the weight of every eye trying to turn my life into a scandal worth talking about.

I shut the door behind me with a soft click and press my palms to the cool marble of the sink.

I don't hear him coming.

"You never did like to be in the spotlight."

I turn.

Chase is standing far too close, all polished edges and expensive cologne meant to mask the tension humming off him. His posture reads composed, collected... but his eyes are anything but. They're too bright, too focused, glinting with barely concealed fury beneath the surface.

"I wasn't trying to take the spotlight. You're right. I hate it," I say, keeping my tone at a careful level. I'm talking down a live wire I don't want to snap.

"No?" He asks, tilting his head. "Because walking in with him? Pretty loud message."

"No," I say quietly. "It wasn't meant to be a message at all."

He laughs bitterly and continues on like I never said anything. "You think this means something to him? That this is about you?"

I narrow my eyes without saying a word.

"He's not here for you, Eden. He's still pissed I married you. This is his way of getting even." His jaw tightens. "He's using you."

"No," I say simply. "You did that. And I let you. I'm not making that mistake twice."

For a second, he doesn't move. Doesn't speak. Something ugly flashes behind his eyes, something that used to scare me.

And before he can say another word, Nash is there.

"You need to leave," Nash says to Chase. He is done playing nice. His tone is hard as granite.

Chase scoffs. "This isn't your business."

Nash's jaw tics. "You're talking to her like she's yours. She's not."

"She's my—"

"She's not your anything," Nash repeats, firmer now.

Chase's smile changes, eyes turning almost black around the edges. "Some choices come with consequences, Eden. I just hope you're ready for yours."

He walks away without another word. But my skin prickles, cold and wrong, like that warning was more than just empty words.

I don't breathe. My hands won't unclench. I keep hearing his voice in my head. Something's coming. I can feel it. I can't help it. I'm scared.

"Are you okay?" Nash asks.

I nod, but it's not convincing.

"I hate that he got to you," he murmurs. His hands going to my head, running his fingers through my hair.

"He didn't," I say. But it's a lie. He's still in my chest, my mind, everywhere really. "I need to not think."

His gaze drops to my mouth, before he lowers his lips to mine. "Say the word."

"Let's do it," I say. "Here and now."

Cold sinks into my skin, but it's not the kind I can shake off. It's in my chest, in my spine. Chase walked away, but he took the air with him.

I don't want to be alone. I don't want to think. I want something that drowns him out.

Nash doesn't say anything when I reach for him. He just pulls me in. Sometimes it's just about forgetting.

The bathroom isn't romantic. It's too bright, too echoey, too close to the sound of clinking glasses and fake laughter. But his mouth finds mine and I stop caring.

He presses me against the door, hard enough to ground

me. I kiss him like I'm chasing something I lost and maybe never had at all. His hands slide under my dress and I gasp.

This isn't about pretty. It's not about being overly sweet. It's about pulling the fear and anger out by the roots.

The rest comes in scattered fragments. His pants drag roughly across my thighs, silk tearing in his fist, lace caught around my ankle.

His teeth scrape the spot below my jaw and I gasp before I can stop it. I bite down on his shoulder through the cotton, anything to keep quiet. We're in public after all.

"Eden," my name escapes like something torn from him, his breath feels like it's scorching against the hollow of my neck beneath my ear where my pulse hammers wildly.

The bathroom door scrapes my bare back as Nash lifts me against it, leaving angry red trails I'll discover tomorrow in my mirror.

His cock pushes into me. His grip shifts, calloused fingertips pressing half moon crescents into the soft flesh of my thighs.

My pussy clenches around him, greedy and demanding after everything that happened with Chase. My crimson nails find the hem of his crisp white shirt, now wrinkled beyond salvation.

We move together like a hurricane just about to meet the shoreline. It is panicked and quick without a second thought for anything around us.

Something electric breaks loose deep inside me, igniting where his cock fills me completely and radiating outward like lightning until I'm clutching him, trembling violently against the cold door.

He follows, coming with a guttural sound that reverberates through my chest cavity as he empties himself inside me, holding me suspended in the air.

He puts me down. I head to the sink and clean up as best as I can. I'm breathless as he gives me a little smile.

I am ready to start my life.

I am allowed to love.

I always thought I knew what it was.

I was wrong.

This is.

CHAPTER THIRTEEN

Nash

I don't mind the mornings anymore.

She's here.

That's enough to know what I want.

Eden suddenly comes down the hall laughing. Her hand is over her mouth, breath gone, shoulders shaking like she's trying not to wake the house.

I look up from my coffee. "That bad?"

She leans on the counter, still smiling.

"She raised no money," she says. "Nash. None." She grins and lifts the phone. "Let me read you the article."

She clears her throat.

"Last night's Valentine's Charity Soirée promised love, community, and generosity," she reads. "What it delivered was champagne, speeches, and zero dollars raised for the cause."

That tracks. It was a charity event, sure. Just one where the money went straight to Chase's campaign. Not someone who actually needed it.

She keeps going. "Guests applauded politely, nodded

enthusiastically, and then exited the venue without opening their wallets."

Polite is Southern for no.

"One attendee reportedly stepped outside to take a phone call during the donation ask."

I saw him do it, too. He didn't even try to act like he was hiding it.

She scrolls, warming to it now. "Despite the live violin-ist, champagne wall, and multiple speeches centered on love and togetherness, the evening failed to generate financial support for a small business grant."

Stated cause. That's a choice.

She laughs under her breath and reads on. "Several guests were overheard asking whether donations were required or if the event was simply a social gathering."

If you have to ask, you already know the answer to that.

She reaches the end, slowing down. "Organizers are calling the night a success based on turnout, atmosphere, and community presence."

That's what folks say when money doesn't show.

She lowers the phone, still smiling like she can't believe it happened.

I take another sip of coffee.

Sunday lunch felt like the right time. Eden is happy and unguarded. Surrounded by people who know her, who stayed around. Not a crowd. Just family. The ones that mean something.

So I asked Willa to come over. I never told her the reason. Only that it's important. She didn't ask why. But she knew since she said she would be there and not to screw this shit up again.

I called Wes next, asking if he could make it. He paused, then said yeah and mentioned calling in Tasha to do the intakes. Of course I told him that he didn't have to. She is always welcome, but she declined saying another time.

I asked my mom too. She didn't hesitate. She's bringing some of our favorites.

Eden thinks it's just lunch with her parents. She's excited to spend some time with them.

She doesn't know I picked today on purpose.

The ring's in my jacket pocket. I keep forgetting about it, then remembering all at once.

I watch her disappear down the hall to change and tell myself this isn't about getting it perfect.

It's about choosing her.

An hour later, we pull into her parents' driveway with the windows cracked and the radio on low. Eden leans forward in her seat, mid-sentence, then trails off as she looks around.

"Huh," she says, glancing toward the side of the house. "That's Willa's car."

I keep my eyes on the wheel.

She looks again.

"And that's Wes's truck," she adds. "Did we miss something."

Her tone is curious but not suspicious. It's a small town. Her parents could have invited everyone over.

"Probably just stopping by," I say, which is technically true.

She smiles to herself. "Of course they are. My parents can't host a meal without half the town wandering in."

She reaches for the door handle before I can stop her.

"Surprise!" It's loud, clumsy, and heartfelt. A group of people who just want to be there for us.

Her mother is right there, already tearing up, hands hovering like she doesn't know whether to laugh or cry. Her dad hangs back a step, trying to act like this is ordinary and failing in all the ways that matter. There's warmth everywhere I look.

Willa's smile is a proud one, the sort that says she's been holding onto this secret for a while. To be fair, she has. Wes gives me a small nod from the corner. He is trying to stay out of the way. My mom stands near the kitchen, watching Eden with a small smile on her face. She's always loved her.

Eden stops just inside the doorway, her smile slips for a second until it brightens up a bit.

She looks at me first, confused. The face of someone who missed the punchline of a joke.

"What is this?" She asks, laughing a little. "Did I forget someone's birthday?"

I step inside and close the door behind us. My heart is beating hard enough that I'm surprised no one can hear it.

"No," I say. "You didn't forget anything."

The room goes quiet without me prompting it to.

I reach into my jacket pocket, and for a second my fingers brush the ring I brought, the one that's waited its turn. I don't pull it out yet.

Instead, I take the bread tie from my pocket.

Her brows knit together as I hold it out between us.

"This was the first ring I ever got from you," I say. "Back when we were nothing but kids."

Her smile wavers.

"I didn't have the nerve then," I say, my voice steady even though my hands are not. "Didn't think I had the right."

Her eyes shine now, and she's stopped laughing entirely.

"I do now."

I slide the bread tie into her palm and close her fingers around it.

"This was the promise," I say. "The one I never got to make."

Then I reach back into my pocket and pull out the ring I chose for her. A simple silver band with a small diamond. It's thoughtful. And exactly her.

"This," I say, holding it up where she can see it clearly, "is me keeping it."

She lets out a small, broken sound that might be my name. Tears spill before she can stop them, and that's when my own chest finally gives in.

"I don't want us to be perfect," I tell her. "I don't want easy. I want you. I want mornings and Sundays and every hard thing in between, if you'll have me."

I take a breath. "Eden Taylor, will you marry me?"

She doesn't answer right away. She just steps into me, forehead against my chest, crying in a way that feels like relief. Her mother is crying too. Willa absolutely is. My mom wipes her eyes and looks proud.

"Yes," Eden says finally, her voice breaking on the word. "Yes, Nash. Always yes."

I slide the ring onto her finger, right next to the bent little promise that came first, and for the first time in my life, everything feels exactly where it belongs.

She laughs through her tears and pulls me down into her, hands fisting in my jacket like she needs to make sure I'm real. I kiss her in a way that shows that it isn't about anyone else in the room. Someone claps. Someone sniffles. I barely hear it.

That's when the front door opens hard.

"I knew it."

Eva's voice cuts through the room. Well now we're all taken out of the moment.

Everyone turns.

She stands in the doorway in last night's dress, the pale silk wrinkled at the waist, heels in her hand, mascara smudged beneath eyes that are too bright to be steady. Her hair is still done, but it's coming out of it's perfect placement strand by strand, the polish slipping the longer she stands there breathing too fast.

She takes in the room in one sweep. Eden's hand in mine. The ring on her finger.

"So this is why no one would answer their phones," she says. "Unbelievable."

No one responds to her.

"You have no idea what I'm dealing with," she says, her voice climbing as she moves farther into the room, heels dangling from her fingers while the hem of last night's dress brushes the floor. "Chase is talking about filing for divorce as if it were a routine business decision, something you schedule and move on from."

She laughs, high and strained, then presses a hand to her chest as though she needs the support.

"I built my entire life around him," she says. "I gave up my name, my time, my reputation, and every ounce of privacy I had to make his campaign work."

She gestures at herself. "I stood beside him when it stopped being charming. When people started questioning him. When he needed someone to smooth things over and keep him presentable."

Still nothing from any of us. We all know this is how Chase is. She's the last to catch up.

A laugh escapes her, thin and edged, carrying none of the ease it pretends to. "He's a liar. A narcissist. He's been awful for our entire marriage and I stayed because someone had to make it work."

Her eyes flick to Eden.

"I guess I should've known," she adds. "You always did have a talent for landing on your feet."

No one rushes to comfort her. No one argues. No one asks what she needs.

"Eva," Eden says, pulling her hand from mine, "you can't lose something that was taken from you."

Eva scoffs, but Eden keeps going before she can interrupt.

"You chose what you chose," Eden says. "You wanted what I had because you thought it would feel different once it was yours. A shiny toy is better when it belongs to someone else. You've always been like that."

Eva's mouth tightens.

"But it never does," Eden continues. "It just looks better from the outside. That's the part no one tells you."

She gestures lightly, not accusatory, just factual. "You stepped into my life thinking it would fix something in you. It didn't. That doesn't make you a victim now. It just means you were wrong."

Eva shakes her head, already defensive. "You have no idea what it's been like."

"I do," Eden says quietly. "I lived it first, remember."

She gasps in mock outrage.

"You don't get to come in here and dismantle what I built from your betrayal because you're unhappy with what you took," Eden says. "I'm done paying for choices that were never mine."

Eden takes a breath, then softens her tone just a fraction.

"I hope you figure out what you actually want someday," she says. "But you will not use me to find happiness. I am not your punching bag."

Eden steps back to my side and takes my hand again, not shaking, not looking away.

That is the moment Eva realizes there is nothing left to win here.

"You need to leave," Ray says.

Eva turns toward him, eyes wide, offended all over again.

"I'm family," she says. "I belong here."

Ray shakes his head once.

"You were not welcome before," he says. "You are not welcome now. You made your choice, Eva."

"But dad—"

"You came in here to look for sympathy for yourself. You wanted to cross a bridge that you burned to the ground with a huge smile on your face," he continues, his voice unimpressed but not surprised. "You did not ask how your sister was. You did not congratulate her. You came to try to convince us who Chase is when we already know."

Eva scoffs, but Ray does not let it derail him.

"You are just as much of a narcissist as Chase is," he says plainly. "You just hide it behind prettier attire."

Eva opens her mouth, then closes it when nothing useful comes to mind.

He gestures toward the door, calm and absolute. "Get out."

She turns for the door. She can't get to it before it slams wider.

Chase comes through the door too fast, breath already off, face flushed and unfocused. His tie is loosened, jacket slipping off one shoulder, the whole thing careless in a way that tells me he didn't stop to think before coming in.

He doesn't register Eva at first.

He doesn't register anyone.

His eyes lock on Eden, and everything else drops out of the room. He notices the ring on her finger, and his face changes in a way I don't like.

"Eden," he says, breathless, forcing his eyes back to her face. "Tell me that ring doesn't mean what I think it does."

No one moves. Eva freezes near the door, forgotten now.

"You need to leave," Ray says.

Chase turns toward him, clearly not expecting resistance from that direction.

"Ray, this doesn't involve you," he says, forcing a thin smile. "This is between me and Eden."

Ray does not raise his voice. He does not move out of the way. "You're standing in my house, boy," he says. "That makes it my business."

Chase exhales sharply, irritation flashing across his face.

"I'm not here to cause a scene," he says. "I just want a conversation."

"You're already causing one," Ray says. "And you're done here."

Chase opens his mouth, then glances at Eden again, desperate to regain control.

"You're really going to let him speak for you," he says to her. "After everything we shared."

Ray doesn't look at Eden. His eyes stay on Chase and Eva. "You heard me," he says. "Get out. Both of you."

"Eden," he says in a way that feels practiced. "Don't do this."

I feel her tense beside me.

"You don't have to decide anything today," he continues, taking a step in her direction despite Ray standing between them. "You're emotional. Anyone would be. This is a lot all at once."

Ray shifts, blocking him fully.

"I'm talking to her," Chase snaps.

Eden finally speaks before Ray can answer. "I already decided," she says, something almost like a laugh escaping her.

Chase shakes his head immediately, refusing it. "No, you didn't," he says. "You're reacting. That's what you do when you feel cornered."

Her hand tightens in mine.

"You loved me," he says, voice rising just enough to carry through the room. He's making sure everyone is listening. Charming in a way that says he can get anything or anyone he wants. "You don't just stop loving someone because things get hard. We had a life. Plans. History."

"You left," Eden says, almost laughing fully now. Letting the ridiculousness of the situation break through her fear. "You chose someone else."

"I made a mistake," he says quickly. "I fixed it. I'm fixing it right now."

He gestures at the room, the people, the ring.

"This is fast," he says. "This isn't you. You don't rush. You think things through."

"I did," she says. "I thought about Nash for years. Seven in fact."

His face tightens, frustration bleeding through all the charm.

"You're really going to throw everything away for him," he says, finally looking at me again. "For someone who couldn't even show up when it mattered."

I step forward, but Eden moves first.

"He stayed away because he respected me. Let me clarify. He respected my choice," she says. "You stayed because you needed me."

Chase laughs right in her face.

"You think this is respect," he says. "He waited until we got divorced. I fought our entire relationship."

"You competed," Eden says. "With everyone. Including me."

"This isn't over," he says, voice low and shaking. "You don't get to erase me."

"I'm not erasing you," Eden says. "I'm done carrying your shit."

That's when I step forward. Enough is enough. Eden doesn't have to say anything.

"You're done," I tell him.

He finally looks at me like I've materialized out of nowhere. His jaw tightens.

"This is between me and my wife," he snaps.

"She's not yours," I say. "You have a wife, for fuck's sake."

He laughs, but there's panic under it now. He looks back at Eden, desperate to get control of the narrative again.

"You really think this lasts," he says. "You think this is love and not just nostalgia?"

"I didn't choose him because he showed up today," she says, voice calm enough to be deadly. "I chose him because he was willing to work on it. All you've ever wanted is an audience full of admirers."

Chase stares at her, breathing hard, something dark rising up where charm used to be.

Willa shifts. Wes steps closer. Eden's father moves without speaking, placing himself just slightly in front of her mother.

Chase notices the walls closing in. The fact that no one is on his side.

Eva laughs, low and bitter.

"Wow," she says. "Now I really get it."

That's when Chase breaks.

"You think you're better than me," he says, voice cracking, eyes locked on me now. "You always did."

He takes another step toward me, too close now, hands shaking.

"You stole my life," he says.

"I didn't take anything," I tell him. "You gave it away."

Something flashes in his eyes.

I recognize it before he opens his mouth. He's about to pull some shit. I know it.

"If I can't have you, Edie," he says, voice breaking open, stripped of all reason, "then no one can."

I see the knife in his hand and the decision already made.

He lunges.

It drives into my side hard, buried deep, the impact knocking the breath straight out of me.

For a split second, nothing hurts.

Then everything does.

Pain blows through me, massive and immediate, ripping low and deep, my legs locking as blood starts pouring out fast enough that I can feel the heat of it soaking my shirt and hand all at once.

This is bad. This is catastrophic.

He yanks it free and drives it back in. I feel the second hit rip through me.

My knees buckle.

I grab his arm and wrench it sideways, the knife tearing out of me with a sound that steals what little breath I had left. Pain explodes through my spine, and I taste blood in my mouth even though I don't remember biting my tongue.

Chase doesn't get another step.

Wes is on him immediately, driving him back into the wall hard enough to shake the pictures. I hear the impact more than I see it. Chase shouts something meaningless as Wes locks him there, forearm across his throat.

Hands reach for me. Eden first.

"Someone call an ambulance," she says, loudly. She's giving instructions she expects to be followed. "Now. Tell them he's been stabbed. Tell them it's bad."

Her hands are back on me, firm pressure at my side, blood soaking through her fingers. She's shaking, but her voice doesn't.

"It's okay," she says, close now, her face filling my vision. "I'm here. You're okay. Stay with me."

The room starts to pull away at the edges, sound stretching thin and distant.

I force my eyes open because I need to see her.

"I told you," I manage, my voice rough and broken, the words dragging themselves out. "I told you I'd love you for the rest of my life."

Her breath catches hard, and she shakes her head like she's refusing the idea of anything else.

"You are," she says. "You're doing that right now. You have a long life ahead of you."

I try to lift my hand. It barely moves, but she catches it anyway, presses it to her chest, right over her heart.

"I meant it," I say. "All of it. Sundays. Mornings. The long way."

She leans down until her forehead rests against mine, tears slipping into my hair.

"I know," she whispers. "I know. Just stay."

Sirens start somewhere far away, or maybe they're already here and I just can't tell.

"I chose you," I tell her, because that part still feels solid. "I'll always choose you."

Her voice breaks when she answers.

"I'm choosing you back," she says. "Every day. So you don't get to go anywhere."

I hold onto that. To her face. To her voice. To the feel of her hands keeping me here.

Everything else fades away.

CHAPTER FOURTEEN

Eden

They load Nash into the ambulance.

I stand close enough that one of the paramedics keeps glancing at me like he's waiting for me to collapse or scream or get in the way. I don't do any of those things. I watch their hands. I watch the blood soak through the gauze faster than they want it to. I watch Nash's face, pale and still, his eyes half lidded but fighting.

"I'm here," I tell him, even though I don't know if he can hear me. "I'm right here."

His fingers twitch when they slide him in. That's enough to keep me upright.

The doors close. The siren doesn't turn on right away, and that scares me more than anything else.

Then I hear the police radio crackle.

Chase is shoved into the back of a cruiser. His hands are cuffed behind him, his shirt streaked with blood that isn't his, his face finally stripped of every version of himself he ever practiced.

"Eden—Eden, you don't understand, this isn't what it

looks like—" He starts to fight the cuffs. "You can't do this to me. Do you know who I am? Get your hands off me."

It is exactly what it looks like.

The door slams shut.

Good.

I hope it finally scares the shit out of him.

My legs finally start shaking once Nash is gone. Willa's hand finds my back before I can slide down the side of my parents' porch.

"Breathe," she murmurs. "Just breathe."

I do. Barely.

That's when I hear Eva.

"You know," she says, too loud for the moment, her voice carrying with that careful cruelty she's always been good at, "this was bound to happen."

I turn slowly.

She's standing near the road, arms folded tight, mascara smeared beneath eyes that look clearer now than they did all night.

"He always had to be the hero," she continues, nodding toward the ambulance disappearing down the road. "Men like Nash don't know when to step aside. This is what happens when they try to win something that was never theirs."

Whatever was holding me back lets go all at once.

I don't remember crossing the distance between us. I just remember her back hitting metal and the sound it makes when it does.

"What are you doing—"

I don't think. I just move. Both my hands close around her throat and drive her back into the car hard enough to make it shake. Whatever she was about to say disappears as her hands claw at my wrists, panic crashing through her like she finally understands she pushed the wrong person.

"You do not get to say his name," I tell her, my voice shaking with something raw and uncontrollable. "You do not get to touch this with your filth."

She chokes, eyes wide.

"You're crazy," she gasps.

"Your *husband* fucking *stabbed* him," I say, my voice cracking around the words. "He put a knife in him. Nash is fighting for his life right now, and you have the nerve to stand here and make it his fault."

Her breathing turns shallow and frantic.

"You married him to beat me," I say. "And now he's fucking ruined everything, so you want to drag me into it with you."

Someone shouts my name. I don't turn.

Then I let go.

Eva slides down the side of the car, coughing hard, dragging in air like she forgot how. Willa is suddenly there, arms around me.

"That's enough," she says softly. "You're done."

I nod once, chest heaving, hands shaking now that the adrenaline has nothing left to hold onto.

I don't look at Eva again.

My eyes go back to the empty road.

Nash is somewhere ahead of me.

I wipe my hands on my jeans, even though the blood doesn't come off, and turn back toward the house.

I can't stay. "I'm going to the hospital," I say, already grabbing my keys and purse.

Willa's with me in two steps. "I'm driving," she says, and doesn't wait for an argument.

Out on the street, doors are slamming. Engines are

turning over. My dad's truck pulls out first, then Nash's mom right behind him. Wes cuts across the driveway as he backs out hard, not careful at all.

The car ride is a blur. I keep replaying the sound of the knife coming out of him, the way his blood soaked into my hands like it was trying to claim me too.

I scrub at my palms on my jeans again.

"Hey," Willa says, glancing at me. "He's tough. You know that."

"I know," I say, even though what I know doesn't help. What I know is how still he went. How heavy. How his eyes stayed on me like I was the only thing keeping him here.

The hospital lights are too bright. They ask me his name, his date of birth, questions I answer without thinking. I can barely stay focused now.

They tell me to wait.

I pace. I sit. I stand again. My knee bounces so hard it rattles the chair. I don't pray. I don't beg. I just stare at the doors and dare them to open.

When they finally do, my heart slams so hard I think it might break something.

"Nash Grady," a nurse says.

I'm on my feet before she finishes the sentence.

The nurse looks from me to the small group that's risen with me, like she's deciding how much she's allowed to say. My chest is tight enough that it's hard to breathe.

"I'm his mother."

Sharon's voice is calm and unwavering as she steps forward, already reaching into her purse for her ID. There is no question in her tone, no room for debate.

"And I'm his fiancée," I say, the word new in my mouth. "I was with him when it happened."

The nurse doesn't hesitate after that. She nods once and motions for us to follow.

The hallway is long and too bright, the kind of sterile white that makes everything feel unreal. I focus on Sharon's back as we walk, the straightness of her shoulders. I stay close enough that I can feel her steadying me without touching. I hope my presence is doing the same for her.

They stop us outside a set of double doors.

"Wait here," the nurse says. "The doctor will come talk to you."

When the doctor finally comes out, he looks tired in the way people do when they've been handling situations that deal with someone else's life.

He introduces himself. I don't catch his name.

"Nash Grady was brought in with multiple stab wounds to the abdomen," he says, looking between Sharon and me. "One penetrated deeply. There was significant blood loss."

My hands curl into fists at my sides.

"We took him into surgery immediately," the doctor continues. "The blade caused internal damage, but we were able to repair what it hit. He lost a lot of blood, but he responded well once we stabilized him."

Sharon exhales slowly, like she's been holding that breath for hours.

"He's alive," I say. It comes out flat. I need to hear it spoken back to me.

"Yes," the doctor says. "He's alive."

My knees threaten to give out, and Sharon's hand closes around my wrist.

"He's still critical," the doctor adds. "The next twenty four hours are important. He's sedated now, but stable. We'll keep him closely monitored."

"Can we see him?" I ask.

The doctor nods. "Briefly. He's in recovery. One at a time."

Sharon looks at me.

"You go first," she says. "He'll want you."

I swallow hard and nod. The nurse opens the door and steps aside, and I walk into a room that smells like antiseptic and something faintly metallic underneath. The lights are dimmer in here.

Nash is in the bed, propped slightly on pillows, tubes and wires everywhere, like the hospital had to remind him who was in charge. His skin looks pale against the white sheets, lashes dark against his cheeks. There's a bandage wrapped tight around his middle, another at his arm, an IV taped into his hand.

He looks too still.

For one terrible second, my chest locks up again.

Then his fingers twitch.

I move closer without thinking, stopping at the edge of the bed like I'm afraid the floor might give way if I lean too hard into this moment. I take his hand carefully, mindful of everything attached to him, and wrap both of mine around it.

"Hey," I whisper, dragging my hands through his hair.

His brow furrows. His lashes flutter. When his eyes finally open, they're unfocused at first, hazel dulled by medication and pain.

Those eyes find me. Everything in his face softens at once.

There's a breathy sound in his chest, almost a laugh, almost a sigh. His fingers tighten weakly around mine, like he's checking that I'm real.

"Told you," he murmurs, voice rough and barely there. "I'd stay."

I press my forehead to his hand, tears spilling over before I can stop them. "You're not allowed to be light about this," I say, my voice breaking anyway. "You scared the hell out of me."

A corner of his mouth lifts.

"Worth it," he says.

I shake my head and laugh through the tears, leaning closer so he doesn't have to strain to see me. "You don't get to do that again," I tell him. "Ever."

His thumb brushes my knuckle, slow and clumsy.

"Wasn't planning on it," he says. "Still got a lot of mornings left."

My throat closes on a sob.

I lift his hand carefully and press my lips to his knuckles, right where his skin is warm and solid and alive. "I'm here," I tell him. "I'm not going anywhere."

His eyes never leave my face.

"Good," he says quietly. "Because I already told the world you're mine."

I smile at that, wide and unguarded and a little wrecked, and lean down so my lips brush his forehead, gentle as a promise.

"I love you," I say.

His eyes slip closed again, exhaustion finally winning, but his grip tightens just enough to let me know he heard me.

"I know," he murmurs. "I chose you."

I stay there, holding his hand, counting his breaths, letting the machines hum and beep and do their jobs. Outside this room, there will be questions and consequences and healing that takes time.

In here, there is only this.

His hand in mine. The steady rise of his chest. The low hum of machines doing the work his body is too tired to do alone. He's asleep now, finally, but his fingers still curl around mine with intention, like letting go is not an option he's willing to consider.

Neither am I.

I trace the line of his knuckles, memorizing the feel of him in this moment, not because I'm afraid of losing it, but because I want to carry it forward. This is what choosing looks like when the noise dies down. This is what love looks like when it survives the worst thing.

I think about the girl I used to be. The one who believed love was loud and shiny and earned through endurance. The one who thought being chosen meant being claimed.

I know better now.

Love isn't loud. It doesn't perform. It steps forward and stays, even when everything else in life feels like it's falling apart.

Sharon appears in the doorway, her presence needed at this moment, and when she looks at me there is no question in her eyes. She's not mad at me. She still loves me too.

I lean down and press my lips to Nash's forehead, trying to be careful of all the cords.

"I'm here," I whisper. "I'm not going anywhere."

His grip tightens, unmistakable this time, even in sleep. It's not just a reflex, but a need.

I smile, because of course it is.

When I finally let go of his hand, it doesn't feel like leaving. It feels like trusting what we've already decided. What we said out loud. What we proved when it counted.

Love doesn't always look like saving someone.

Sometimes it looks like surviving together.

Sometimes it looks like choosing again after everything breaks.

Sometimes it looks like knowing, without doubt, that this is the life you want.

I turn off the light before I go, leaving him wrapped in the love of everyone near us.

I don't wonder if love is real. I never will again.

I chose it, and this time, it chose me back.

Epilogue
WILLA

It's been a month since Nash got home from the hospital, which means life has officially decided to act like none of us were traumatized.

Ink & Stem is back to normal. Orders stacked by the register. Dried petals everywhere no matter how often I sweep. Eden at the big table by the window, sleeves rolled up, ink on her fingers, pretending she's not the emotional center of the universe.

Nash is sitting on the stool next to her, one hand braced on the table, the other wrapped around a coffee he absolutely should not still be drinking. He looks better. Still healing, still moving carefully, but solid now. Even more annoying than before as well.

Eden finishes a line, sets her pen down, and exhales like she's been holding her breath since she started.

"I need to tell you something," she says.

I don't even look up from trimming stems. "If this is about how you reorganized the ink shelf again, I swear to God—"

"I'm pregnant."

The shears slip in my hand and clatter onto the counter.

I look up slowly. "I'm sorry. What?"

Nash chokes on his coffee.

Eden winces. "Okay, maybe I should've eased into that."

"You think," I say. "You think maybe that's not a casual before lunch sentence."

Nash is staring at her like she just informed him gravity stopped working. "You're—" He stops. Starts again. "We're—"

"Yes," Eden says. "Apparently."

I point my shears at her. "Wow. Incredible. Really love that I'm finding out at the *same time* as the man who helped make the baby."

Eden winces. "Okay, when you say it like that—"

"I'm saying it exactly like that," I tell her. "You couldn't give him a heads up. A text. A smoke signal."

Nash blinks. "Wait, you knew before me?"

"I found out thirty seconds ago," I say. "And somehow I'm still offended on your behalf."

Eden sighs. "I panicked." She grimaces. "I took three tests."

Nash looks like he might faint.

I point a finger at him, raising my brow. "Sit down your ass back down before you face plant. I do not have fiancé hits head on worktable on my bingo card."

He sits. Immediately. Smart man.

"How long have you known?" I ask.

"Since this morning," Eden says. "I was going to wait. I didn't wait."

"You never wait," I tell her. "It's your brand."

Nash drags a hand down his face. "I got stabbed," he says slowly. "And now this."

Eden snorts. "You survived."

"I know," he says. "I just didn't expect the sequel this fast."

I lean back against the counter and really look at them. Eden is nervous but glowing in that way that says she's excited and terrified. Nash is stunned and already completely in it.

"Well," I say, picking my shears back up while I smirk at my best friend, "congratulations. You're officially doing life on hard mode."

Eden smiles. Nash laughs, a little hysterical, a little awed.

"Are you okay?" He asks her, finally finding his footing.

She nods. "I am. I think I just needed to say it out loud."

"You did," I say, laughing in her face. "With witnesses. Bold choice."

Nash reaches for her hand, careful like always now, and she lets him, threading their fingers together without even looking.

The bell over the door jingles. Nice break from the drama, if I must say.

"Well, I'll be damned if this place don't smell expensive today."

Hal Perkins ambles in like time is optional, mail satchel slung over one shoulder, ball cap older than me and probably tougher too. He's been delivering mail in this town since the dinosaurs walked the earth.

"Morning, Hal," I say, smiling. "You're late."

He squints at the clock on the wall. "Clock's wrong."

It isn't.

He pulls out a small stack of envelopes, flips through

them with exaggerated care, then holds one up between two fingers like it might bite.

"Got a card for you, Willa," he says. "Handwritten. Fancy paper. Whoever sent it spent money."

I narrow my eyes. "That's never good."

He chuckles and sets it on the counter. Then he pulls out another envelope. Same black paper. Same weight. Same everything as one I've seen before.

"I delivered a card like this to Eden," he adds, glancing over his glasses at her.

My stomach drops.

Eden freezes.

Nash's head snaps up.

Hal clears his throat, suddenly aware of the room in a way he wasn't a second ago. "Anyway," he says, backing toward the door, "y'all have a blessed day."

The bell jingles again as he leaves.

I turn slowly and see it sitting on the counter near Eden's elbow. Black envelope. No return address. Heavy paper.

Eden looks at it. Then at me.

"Well," she says carefully, "shit, sis."

Nash frowns. "What is that?"

I don't answer him. I keep my eyes on the envelope.

Eden nudges it toward me with one finger. "Looks like it's your turn for a creepy Valentine's Day threat."

Up Next

Up Next in the Almost: A Dark Valentine Series
Willa and Wes were never done.
They were just unfinished.
Now a Valentine card shows up with her name on it.
And Willa knows better than to believe in coincidences.
Almost Mine
Coming June 25, 2026

Up Next in the Devil's Bargain Series
He's never been in a hurry for anything.
She's spent her whole life giving too much to everyone else.
But Sloth isn't about to wait.
He's about to take his time... because he refuses to destroy something beautiful.
Enemies will return. The world is about to fracture.
Coming March 2026

Want More?

Want more of Nash and Eden?
See how they find out the gender of their baby!
Read it here: https://dl.bookfunnel.com/3uruvhcv2h

About the Author

Sara McClaflin writes romance with feelings, flaws, and just the right amount of emotional damage. Her stories are character-driven, morally gray, and often ask one very important question: what if love was a little dangerous—and we liked it that way? After years of reading and reviewing books with too much angst, she finally started writing her own.

She lives on the West Coast with her husband, their chaotic dog, and more book boyfriends than she's willing to admit. Her TBR pile is a cry for help, her playlists are 80%

heartbreak, and she's always chasing the next character who'll ruin her in the best way.

Newsletter Sign-Up

https://subscribepage.io/saranewsletter

Amazon Author Page

https://www.amazon.com/stores/Sara-McClaflin/author/B0CR8VHBHJ

Instagram

https://www.instagram.com/authorsaramcclaflin

Facebook

https://www.facebook.com/profile.php?id=61551822185090

TikTok

https://www.tiktok.com/@sara.mcclaflin

Goodreads

https://www.goodreads.com/author/show/47632250.Sara_McClaflin

Threads

https://www.threads.com/@authorsaramcclaflin

Also By

The Devil's Bargain
Wicked Union– A prequel novella (Liora and Evander's Story)
The Devil's Canvas
Gilded Lies
Unholy Vows (Selene and Theron's Story)
The Shadow Brides
Veil of Fire
Wildflowers & Whiskey (Frankie and Beckett's Story)
The Damaged Bride
The Huntington Brothers Series
Destined for Love
Tangled Hearts
Promises to Keep
Almost: A Dark Valentine
Almost Chosen
Standalone Novels
The Keeper's Secret
Love on the Edge
Anthologies

Head in the Clouds: A Romantic Comedy Anthology
Desperate: A Deadly Thriller Anthology
***

Did you love *Almost Chosen*? If you enjoyed the story, I would be so grateful if you took a moment to leave a quick review. Thank you for reading, for your support, and for spending time with these characters. I can't wait for you to see what happens next!

Content Warning

- Infidelity
  - Spousal cheating with a sibling
  - Sibling betrayal
  - Divorce
  - Sudden abandonment
  - Emotional abuse (non-graphic)
  - Gaslighting
  - Emotional manipulation
  - Victim-blaming
  - Toxic family dynamics
  - Small-town social shaming
  - Anxiety and panic responses
  - Emotional distress
  - Violence
  - Stabbing (non-graphic but on-page)
  - Blood / injury
  - Strong language